"There's more to a relationship than…sex," Katie said.

"Indeed there is, but I think you'll find most men—and women—want the pleasure of enjoying and arousing their chosen partner's sexual desires. You must have experienced that for yourself."

She made no response other than tensing in Sebastian's grasp.

"You have experienced it, haven't you, Katie?" he asked her softly.

"What I have or have not experienced is no concern of yours."

"Perhaps not," Seb agreed, but instead of releasing her and turning away as she had expected, he suddenly moved closer to her, causing her stomach to turn in anxious protest. He bent his head and his mouth came down expertly and inescapably over hers.

"No…" she managed to protest sharply.

"You're a liar, Katie, if what you say you want is a gentle, passive lover," she heard him telling her savagely. "You want a man whose passion matches your own."

Dear Reader,

Penny Jordan continues her dramatic family
saga, THE CRIGHTONS, with *A Perfect Night*.
Here we meet Katie Crighton, who has been
persuaded to return home. With her twin sister
happily married (Louise's story was told in
The Perfect Lover), Katie's wanting to find the
right man and settle down. Someone gentle
and considerate. So why does the dangerously
attractive Sebastian Cooke tantalize her every
thought?

All of the books featuring the Crighton family
can be read independently of each other, as each
tells its own fascinating story, but if you wish to
read the whole collection, then these are the
novels to look for:

Penny Jordan

A PERFECT NIGHT

THE CRIGHTONS

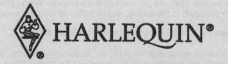

HARLEQUIN®

TORONTO • NEW YORK • LONDON
AMSTERDAM • PARIS • SYDNEY • HAMBURG
STOCKHOLM • ATHENS • TOKYO • MILAN • MADRID
PRAGUE • WARSAW • BUDAPEST • AUCKLAND

ISBN 0-373-12104-0

A PERFECT NIGHT

First North American Publication 2000.

This edition published by arrangement with Harlequin Books S.A.

Visit us at www.eHarlequin.com

Printed in U.S.A.

The Crighton Family

Haslewich branch of the family

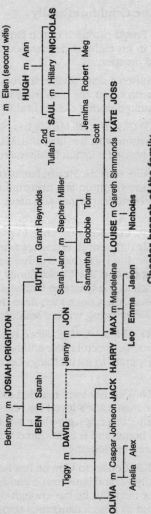

Bethany m JOSIAH CRIGHTON ———————————— m Ellen (second wife)

```
                                                    HUGH m Ann
BEN m Sarah       RUTH m Grant Reynolds                           SAUL m Hillary   NICHOLAS
                                                            2nd
     Jenny m JON                                       Tullah m
                      Sarah Jane m Stephen Miller                    Jemima Robert Meg
Tiggy m DAVID                                                     Scott
                          Samantha  Bobbie  Tom
         HARRY      MAX m Madeleine        LOUISE m Gareth Simmonds   KATE  JOSS

OLIVIA m Caspar Johnson  JACK      Leo  Emma  Jason        Nicholas

  Amelia  Alex
```

Chester branch of the family

```
                                          WILLIAM CRIGHTON m Sophie

                                                HENRY m Patricia

                                  RACHEL LUKE m Bobbie   JAMES ALISON

EDWARD CRIGHTON m Jessica                            Francesca Mark

     LAURENCE m Celia

ALISTAIR NIALL KIT
```

The Crighton Family

BEN CRIGHTON: Proud patriarch of the family, a strong-minded character in his eighties, determined to see his dynasty thrive and prosper.

RUTH REYNOLDS: Ben's sister, a vibrant woman now happily reunited with Grant, the man from whom she was tragically separated during the Second World War.

MADDY AND MAX CRIGHTON: Maddy has blossomed since the reconciliation with her husband, Max, who has finally proved himself a loving family man.

JON AND JENNY CRIGHTON: Steady, family-oriented couple. Jon keeps the Crighton law firm running smoothly with his business partner and niece, Olivia Crighton.

CHRISSIE AND GUY COOKE: Guy, once in partnership with Jenny, is totally different in character from his gentle wife, Chrissie. But their marriage has proved to be a loving and happy one. The Cooke family is as well-known in Haslewich as the Crighton family is. With their Gypsy ancestors, the Cooke men have the notorious reputation of being wicked seducers.

LOUISE AND GARETH SIMMONDS: Since her marriage, a gulf has developed between Louise and her twin, Katie. Louise is desperate to mend things between them.

KATIE CRIGHTON: With her twin married to the gentle, considerate man Katie's loved for years, she has fought shy of family gatherings. Now she has had the courage to return home, and is confronted with a man who stirs every deep-felt longing.

SEBASTIAN COOKE: Cousin to Guy, he has had to overcome his family's scandalous image and is now a successful, wealthy man. But he has enough of the Cooke genes in him to pose a dangerous sexual challenge to Katie Crighton.

CHAPTER ONE

As SEB drove past the sign that read, Haslewich—Please Drive Carefully, he was aware of a dispiriting grey cloud of self-criticism and disappointment dulling what, if life mirrored fiction, by rights should be his triumphal return to the place of his birth.

He was thirty-eight years old, virtually at the top of his career ladder having just been headhunted by the international drug company Aarlston-Becker to head their research team. No small feat surely for man who, as a boy, had been sneeringly dismissed by one of his teachers as 'just another hopeless by-product of the Cooke clan.'

He had money in the bank accumulated by hard work and shrewd investment, a family who even if he hadn't seen much of them in recent years were by all accounts more than willing to do the modern equivalent of roasting a fatted calf to welcome him home, and he was about to take a kind of professional post that many among his colleagues would have given their eye-teeth for; all of which surely must be pretty heavyweight pluses on anyone's balance sheet of life.

But then he *needed* some heavyweight assets to balance out the equally, to him at least, heavyweight negative aspects of his life.

'What negative aspects?' his second or was it third cousin Guy Cooke had asked him drily when they had been discussing the subject of his impending return.

'How about an ill-judged early marriage followed predictably, I suppose, by a divorce.'

Guy's eyebrows had lifted as he shrugged dismissively, 'Divorce isn't exactly a social sin any longer Seb, and from what you've told us your ex-wife has remarried very happily and the two of you are on relatively comfortable terms.'

'Oh yes, from Sandra's and my own point of view the divorce was the best thing we could have done other than not to have married in the first place.

'No, it's not the fact that we married far too young and for all the wrong reasons that I feel bad. It's...' He had paused, grimacing before continuing, 'Sandy always used to complain that I was a selfish bastard not really fit to be either a husband or a father, too wrapped up in my career and my own professional goals. I thought at the time that she was being ridiculous. After all, I was working to provide a decent standard of living for her, or so I used to tell her and myself, but of course that was just the excuse I used to conceal the fact that she was right that I *was* being selfish, and that the rush I got from knowing I was right in there at the cutting edge of discovering new drugs that were going to provide the kind of breakthrough that would change the world was far more important to me, far more compelling and addictive than any pleasure I got from being with her.'

Guy and Chrissie, his wife, had exchanged ruefully happily married looks while Chrissie had lifted their son Anthony up off the floor to give him a hug, and although they had both made the right kind of protestingly reassuring noises Seb hadn't been deceived. Of course privately they must both have thought that he had been selfish. How could they think otherwise? Seb had seen the loving commitment Guy was making to his own family, had witnessed at first hand during his stay with them when he had attended his initial interview the 'hands on' fathering that Guy was giving his son.

'But at least you and Charlotte have formed a proper father and daughter bond now,' Chrissie had reminded him gently.

'Yes, more thanks to Charlotte's maturity than any good parenting on my part,' Seb had returned, adding, 'After all she could very easily have refused to see me when I wrote and asked her if she would consider allowing me back into her life. George, Sandra's second husband has been far more of a proper father to her than I have.'

'Maybe so from a practical point of view,' Guy had agreed, 'But biologically *you* are her father and you only have to see the two of you together to see that.'

'Oh yes, she's got my genes when it comes to her physical looks,' he agreed.

'And she's got your brains by all accounts too,' Chrissie had laughed.

'Well, Sandra and I met originally at university so I suppose that aspect of her nature is down to both of us, but I admit that I was surprised when she told me that she intends to follow much the same career path as I've chosen.'

'And since she's going to be studying for her A levels at a private sixth-form college near Manchester, you're bound to be able to see a lot more of her.'

'I hope so,' Seb had agreed. 'Although at sixteen she's almost an adult now with her own life and her own friends. Sandra did say though that she was relieved to know that I would be on hand for her at the weekends especially now that Sandra and George are likely to be based abroad for the foreseeable future.'

'Well we certainly loved meeting Charlotte,' Chrissie had told him warmly. 'Although I suspect she felt a little bit overwhelmed by the massed ranks and fervent curiosity of the Cooke clan in force.'

The Cooke clan. How he had hated and chafed under the burdensome weight of his family's reputation when he had been growing up, Seb reflected now. Of course he hadn't known then that he wasn't on his own and that Guy, too, had suffered his own personal war between his inner needs and the town's expectations. But then Guy had met Chrissie and in helping her to make peace with her family history Guy had come to terms with his own unhappy childhood memories.

Seb knew that without the incentive of having Charlotte at college in nearby Manchester there was no way *he* would have come back to his birthplace in the small historical Cheshire town where, or so the story went, his family line had come into being following the seduction of a local girl by a member of a notorious band of Romany travellers who visited the town every year.

The children—the *clan*—that union had given birth to down through the centuries, whether rightly or wrongly, had garnered a notorious reputation in the town for not always walking on the right side of the law, and of course predictably it had often been a case of 'give a dog a bad name...' Certainly it seemed that historically, their family had been a convenient peg for the townspeople to hang all their local crimes of theft and unlawfulness on.

Now, of course, those days were gone and his relatives so far as Seb knew were, in the main, sturdy and worthy citizens, and so intermarried and interwoven with the families and fabric of the area that they could not in all fairness any longer be considered to be a separate and dangerously untrustworthy clan of outsiders.

Even so the lusty lifestyle of the original ancestors had left its mark on the collective conscience of the other families in the town. Cooke men had a reputation for fathering sturdy sons whose dark eyes tended to hold the kind of gleam that mothers and young impressionable girls quite rightly found dangerous.

Seb had known from an early age that he wanted to escape from the restrictions of living in a small-town community where everyone knew everyone else. He had wanted to break through the glass ceiling imposed on him by the expectations and reservations of those around him simply because of the surname he carried. It had been his interest, cultivated and encouraged by his grandfather and a fascination with the problems that manifested themselves in the plants his grandfather grew because of their genetic make up which had initially led to his choice of career.

University might have freed him from the restrictions imposed on him by his small-town upbringing but in order to get there he had had to focus on the more self-absorbed, self-interested side of his personality and that ultimately had created a blinkered concentration on his career to the detriment of his personal relationships.

It had taken a comment he had overheard from a female colleague to make him realise the error of his ways. She had been talking with another co-worker unaware that he was in an adjacent room and could hear them.

'He actually hasn't seen his daughter in over ten years. Can you believe that?'

'It happens,' the other woman had pointed out. 'Divorced men *do* lose touch with their children.'

'Yes, I know, but he just doesn't seem to care. Doesn't he have any human feelings?'

That night at home alone in his empty executive apartment Seb had replayed the overheard conversation in his head and he had asked himself the same question.

The answer had shocked him.

Yes, he did care, more than he had known, and he had cared even more after that first fateful reunion with Charlotte when he had recognised not just in her face, her physical features, but in her personality as well, such a strong resemblance to him that he had felt as though someone, something, some emotion, was cracking his heart in a vise.

It had not been an easy task building bridges that would allow them, allow her, to lower the guard she had quite naturally put up against him. She'd been outwardly pleasant and friendly, but he had nevertheless known that inwardly she was extremely wary of him. And who could blame her? But that had been three years ago, and now he was very much a part of her life. But he was still aware that nothing, no amount of remorse, or regret could totally eradicate the past.

Sandra, his ex-wife, had gone on to have two more children, both boys, with her second husband George and Charlotte was very much a part of that happy close-knit family, but she *was* also his daughter and, like him, a Cooke.

'All these relatives,' she had marvelled laughingly when she had visited the town with him. 'I can't believe it. We seem to be related to half the population.'

'At least,' Seb had agreed drily, but unlike him Charlotte seemed to delight in her heritage.

'Things have changed,' Guy had told him. 'There's

been a large influx of new people into the town, opening it up, broadening both its boundaries and its outlook.

'The women of the Cooke family have always had a special strong grittiness and that's really showing itself now. There are Cooke women on the town council, running their own businesses, teaching their children that their inheritance is one to be proud of. Yes, of course, a proportion of the babies at Ruth Crighton's mother and baby home *are* Cookes but on their *fathers'* side and not their mothers'. Cooke girls are hard-working and determined, university and self-fulfilment is *their* goal...'

Seb knew all about the Crightons. Who living in Haslewich *didn't*? Like the Cooke's, the Crighton name was synonymous with the town even though they were relative newcomers to it having only arrived there at the turn of the century.

Chrissie was in part a Crighton although that fact hadn't been realised even by Chrissie's own parents until she'd become involved with Guy.

Jon Crighton was the senior partner in the family's law firm. Olivia, his niece, the daughter of his twin brother David, was also a partner. David himself was someone who was surrounded by mystery, having left the town, some said under highly dubious circumstances. Jon and David's father lived in a large Elizabethan house outside the town along with Max Crighton, Jon and Jenny's eldest son, and his wife and children.

Max was the apple of his grandfather's eye and, to Ben Crighton's pride, was no mere solicitor but a barrister, working from chambers in Chester alongside Luke and James Crighton, sons of Ben's cousin Henry.

The Crighton family had originated from Chester, but a family quarrel had led Josiah Crighton, Ben's father, to move away from Chester and set up his own legal practice in Haslewich, and until relatively recently a certain degree of rivalry had existed between the two branches of the family.

Jenny Crighton, Jon's wife had once owned and run an antiques business in Haslewich in which Seb's cousin Guy had been a partner, but the pressure of her own family commitments had led to her giving up her share in the business, which Guy had kept on as a sideline.

Guy had, in fact, recommended Jon Crighton to Seb as someone to deal with the legal conveyancing side of his house purchase when he moved back into the area.

As yet Seb hadn't found a property he wanted to buy and so instead he was renting somewhere.

'Local property prices are high,' Guy had warned him, 'Thanks to Aarlston-Becker. Not that we can complain, they've brought prosperity to the area even though there are those who claim that their presence threatens the town.'

Seb changed gear as the traffic slowed to a crawl as he entered the town proper. He had thought that in rebuilding his relationship with Charlotte he had laid to rest the guilt he had felt at his shortcomings as a father, but returning to Haslewich had brought back some painful memories.

'What you need Dad, is to fall in love,' Charlotte had told him several months earlier, and even though she had laughed Seb had seen in her eyes that she had been semiserious.

'Falling in love is for people of your age,' he had told her drily.

'Why have you never married again?' she had asked him quietly.

'Do you really need to ask?' Seb had returned sardonically. 'After all, you've had first-hand experience of the mess I made of it the first time. No Lottie,' he had shaken his head, 'I'm too selfish, too set in my ways. Falling in love isn't for me.'

'No you're not, you *just think* you are,' Charlotte had told him, adding with surprising maturity, 'You're just punishing yourself, Dad, because you feel guilty about me. Well, you needn't. I wasn't even two when you and Mum split up, and she and George were together by the time I was three. At least I never experienced the trauma of being torn between you and Mum, and she told me that that was thanks to you agreeing to let George bring me up.'

'So what are you saying…that I did you a favour by turning my back on my responsibility towards you,' Seb had asked her grimly. 'That my selfishness was almost praiseworthy…'

'No, of course not, but at least you did come to feel ultimately that as father and daughter we *should* be part of one another's lives. At least I do know that you love me,' she had added in a soft whisper.

Love her. Yes he did—now—but if he was honest with himself there had been years of her life when he had scarcely allowed himself to remember that she existed and he would carry the burden of that guilt for the rest of his life. Marry again? Fall in love? He cursed abruptly as just in front of him a young woman started across the road without looking causing him to stamp his foot down hard on the brakes. As his car screeched to a halt in front of her she froze in fear, her face turned towards him.

Seb had a momentary impression of her shocked expression, wide eyes set in a piquantly-shaped delicately feminine face, her hair tousled by the light breeze. Small and slender she was wearing a soft, brown linen wrap-

around skirt, the pale colour of the cream silk top tucked
into it complementing both the warmth of the skirt and
the even more alluring light tan of her bare arms—and
legs. But as his brain mentally digested these peripheral
visual facts, the feeling, the emotion uppermost in Seb's
mind was one of anxiety fuelled by anger.

What on earth had possessed her to step right out in
front of him like that? Didn't she realise how close she
had come to causing an accident. The narrow town street
was busy with shoppers and if his brakes had failed to
work so swiftly or if he had skidded...or not been able
to stop... And yet as the shock faded from her eyes, it
wasn't guilt or gratitude he could see replacing it, but
rather a sharply condemnatory anger, as though he were
the one to blame for what was quite patently her foolishness. Indeed, for a second it almost seemed as though
she was about to walk right up to his car instead of
finishing her journey across the busy street, but then the
car driver behind him, growing impatient with the delay,
tooted his horn and she hesitated and then turned aside,
shooting him a searing look before marching stiffly away
from him.

Just as equally infuriated by her behaviour as she
seemed to have been by his, Seb shot her departing back
a fulminating look of male contempt for her female foolishness before slipping the car back into gear and continuing with his journey.

As Katie walked through Haslewich's busy main thor-
oughfare she was aware of a heavy weight of unhappi-
ness dulling what, by rights, should have been a joyous
and hopefully positive return to the bosom of her family.

She was twenty-four years of age, in excellent health,
a fully qualified solicitor who had been not just asked,

but beseeched by her father and her cousin to join them in the family partnership in their home town. Indeed she had even had the satisfaction of having her elder brother no less, add his persuasive arguments to those of the other members of the family.

'Dad needs you Katie,' Max had told her. 'They're absolutely inundated with work, and we all know how grandfather would react if Dad were to suggest taking on a non-Crighton partner, just as we all know that no solicitor worth his or her salt would join the partnership without the expectation of being offered their own partnership. For you to come home and join Dad and Olivia would be the ideal solution to the problem. You're young in terms of legal experience at the moment, but a partnership in the not too distant future is assured.'

'Yes, I daresay it is,' Katie had agreed quietly. 'But you seem to forget Max that I already have a job.'

'I know you do,' Max had agreed, 'but I'm not completely blind Katie, something's gone wrong in your life. Look, I'm not going to pry or ask questions, God knows I don't have the right to act the big brother with you now, after all I was hardly a caring one to you when you and Louise were growing up. What I will say to you, though, is that some people need to seek solitude, to lick their wounds and heal themselves, and others need the care and comfort of their close family, and we both know which camp you fall into.'

It was true, Louise, Katie's twin sister was more the type to seek the solitude Max had just described than her, but then Louise was hardly likely to need to do so. Louise after all was blissfully in love with and loved by Gareth.

Louise and Gareth.

Katie had closed her eyes thankful that no one had

guessed her shameful poisonous secret. It made no difference that she had loved Gareth quietly and sedately and from a distance a long time before Louise had realised the exact nature of her feelings for him. And the reason it made no difference was not just because Louise was her other half, her dearly beloved if sometimes somewhat headstrong and exasperating twin, but because Gareth himself did not love her… Gareth loved Louise.

Stoically Katie had accepted the agonising searing burn of her own pain, claiming pressure of work for her increasingly infrequent visits home and her even more infrequent get-togethers with her twin, but then as though fate had not done enough she discovered that it had another blow in store for her.

Her boss, for whom she had worked ever since she had joined the legal department of the charity to do her articles after leaving university, had resigned, and the man who had taken his place…

Katie closed her eyes in midstep. Jeremy Stafford had at first seemed so charming, so very much on her own wavelength that even now she couldn't properly come to terms with what had happened.

When he had started asking her to work late, she had done so willingly, enjoying not just the rapport between them but the knowledge that the work they were doing was ultimately benefiting people who were so very desperately in need of help.

The first time Jeremy had suggested dinner as a ''reward'' to them both for their hard work, she had felt nothing but pleasure, no sense of wariness or suspicion had clouded her happy acceptance of his suggestion. How naive she had been, but then from the way that Jeremy had always talked about his wife and small children she had assumed that he was so happily married that any kind of betrayal of his wife and their marriage vows—well, it had simply never crossed her mind that it might have crossed his... But she had been wrong...not only had it crossed his, it had lingered there and quite unequivocally taken up a very lustful and leering residence as she had so unpleasantly discovered.

At first when he had started to compliment her on her face and then her figure she had simply assumed that he was being pleasant, but then had come the night when he had put his arm around her when they were leaving the restaurant and then attempted to kiss her.

She had fobbed him off immediately, but to her consternation instead of apologising as she had expected him to do he had turned on her claiming that she had led him on; that she was a tease and worse, oh yes, much much worse. Of course after that there had been no more intimate dinners and no evenings working late, instead there had been hostility and even victimisation: accusations about missing reports which she knew she had filed, mistakes which she knew she had not made, errors which she knew were simply not hers.

Not that she had any intention of telling Max any of that. The change her elder brother had undergone following the attack he had suffered on a Jamaican beach while he was in that country trying to trace their father's missing twin brother, David Crighton, had not merely converted him into a passionately devoted husband and father, it had also turned him into a surprisingly caring and concerned brother and son. If Max guessed for one moment what was going on, Katie knew that he would lose no time in seeking out Jeremy Stafford and demanding retribution for his behaviour.

Had they been children still involved in playground jealousies and quarrels that might just have been acceptable, but they were adults. She was supposed to be in charge of her own life. As a modern independent woman she was expected to be able to deal with her own problems. The sadness was, she loved her work, loved knowing that what she was doing no matter how small, was a benefit to other people.

The Crighton women carried a strong gene of responsibility and duty towards their fellow men and women. In her great-aunt, Ruth Crighton, it had manifested itself in the establishment of an enclave of charitably run accommodation units for single parents and their children. In her mother, Jenny, it showed in the way she gave so much of her time and energy to others. Katie's sister had become involved in a programme to help young drug addicts in Brussels where she and Gareth lived and worked.

Katie froze as the sudden sharp screech of a car's brakes brought her back to reality.

Without realising what she was doing she had started across the road without looking properly, but that in no way excused the manic dangerousness of the speed at which the driver of the car, now stopped in front of her, had to have been driving to have been forced to halt with such a screech. Katie knew nothing about cars and the fact that the very powerful engine of the Mercedes the man was driving was responsible for the intensity of his braking rather than his speed was therefore completely lost on her. Instead what she was aware of was the look of totally unwarranted fury in his eyes as he glowered ferociously out of the car at her.

As her own shock held her motionless she was distantly aware of the fact that he was outrageously good-looking with thick, virtually jet-black, well-groomed hair, chillingly icy grey eyes and a mouth that even when clamped grimly closed still betrayed the fact that he had a disturbingly full and sexy bottom lip.

But none of that compensated for the fact that he had nearly run her over. Determinedly Katie took a step towards the car and then stopped as the driver behind him hooted impatiently. Much as she longed to give Mr Sexy Mouth a piece of her mind, she really didn't have time. She was due at the office ten minutes ago, hardly a good start to her first official working day with her father and Olivia.

It had been a wrench leaving her job, despite the problem she had suffered with Jeremy and she still wasn't sure she had made the right decision in agreeing to join the family practice. Both her father and Olivia had held out the inducement, as Max had already indicated, that in time she could expect to become a full partner, even if right now she was simply being retained by them as a salaried employee. Money had never motivated Katie, but then to be fair she knew that it didn't motivate either her father or Olivia either.

She was to start by taking over the conveyancing side of the business, the legal work attached to the buying and selling of properties. She had pulled a small face when her father had told her this.

'Well at least I should have some practice by the time it comes to my buying my own home,' she had told him ruefully.

Although her parents had offered her back her childhood room permanently, after several years of living independently at the University and then in London, she had felt that it would be more sensible to find her own separate accommodation. In London she had rented and while she waited for the right property to buy to present itself to her at home, she had, just temporarily she had told them, moved back in with her parents.

It had felt distinctly odd to be back in her old room—without her twin.

Louise had been more excited about Katie's decision to return to Haslewich than she had herself; trying to cajole her into a flying visit to Brussels to spend the week with them before Katie took up her new duties.

'Why don't you go?' her father had asked her when he had learned via Jenny of her decision to turn down Louise's invitation.

There wasn't any logical explanation she could give and she had been grateful to her younger brother Joss and her cousin Jack for creating a small diversion as they both pleaded with Jon to be allowed to take up Louise's offer in her stead.

Since it was Joss's all important GCSE year Katie had well been able to understand her father's refusal to agree until after his exams were over and loyally Jack, who was two years older than his cousin, had announced that he didn't want to go until they could both go together.

The pair of them were almost as close as the pairs of twins the Crighton family produced with such regularity, Jack having made his home with Katie's parents after the break-up of his own parents' marriage and the disappearance of his father David.

Ten minutes later, as Katie walked into her father's office after a brief knock on the door, she apologised.

'Sorry I'm late… I'd forgotten how busy the town is and I couldn't find a close by parking spot…'

'Mmm…if you think *this* morning is busy just wait until market day,' her father warned her good-humouredly.

'Olivia won't be here until ten,' he added. 'During

term time she does the morning school and nursery run. Caspar picks the children up in the afternoon.'

Caspar, Olivia's American husband, held a Chair at a nearby university where he lectured in corporate law and it had been while she was on a course that Olivia had met and fallen in love with him.

'It can't be easy for her, working full-time with two young children,' Katie commented.

'No, it isn't,' her father agreed, adding briskly, 'We've cleared out a room for you to use and I've organised some preliminary file reading for you. We'll start you off on some straightforward conveyancing...'

'That's fine,' Katie responded absently.

'Is something wrong?' he asked, sensing her preoccupation.

'Not really...not unless you count nearly being run down by some speed-crazed driver,' Katie told him, briefly explaining what had happened.

'Mmm...it has been mooted that the town be made a no traffic area, but...'

'But...' Katie raised her eyebrows. The town had been there before the Romans, its surrounding salt making it a highly prized asset. The Normans had built a castle which the Roundheads virtually destroyed during the Civil War, and the town's streets dated in the main from the Middle Ages and were consequently narrow and tortuous and certainly not designed for the volume of modern-day traffic that used them.

'Well in order to make that a viable proposition, a new ring road would have to be built, and you can just imagine the cost of it...'

'Mmm...but if it keeps drivers like Mr Sexy Mouth off the road...'

'Like who?' her father questioned.

Katie flushed a little. Now what on earth had prompted her to use that particular description of him out loud?

'Er… Nothing,' she denied hastily, quickly turning her attention to the files her father was showing her.

CHAPTER TWO

'JENNY Crighton is giving an informal supper party in a few weeks' time,' Guy gave his cousin the date, 'and she's invited you to go along with us, Seb. You'll enjoy it,' he encouraged when he saw the way Seb was frowning.

He had called round to see him expressly to deliver Jenny's invitation as well as to see how his cousin had settled in at Aarlston-Becker.

'Shall I?' Seb challenged him.

'Which reminds me,' Guy added before Seb could continue, 'Chrissie said to tell you that you're more than welcome to come round and dine with us any time you wish.'

'Thanks, I really do appreciate the offer, but right now I'm so involved at work...' Seb stopped and shook his head. Despite his misgivings about returning to the town of his birth, Seb had to admit that the sheer scope of the work he was involved with at Aarlston was proving enormously challenging and satisfying. The company was right at the forefront of research into and the creation of a new generation of drugs.

'I had planned to drive over to Manchester that weekend to see Charlotte, but it seems she's organised to go away with a group of friends, which means...'

'Which means that you'll be free to accept Jenny's invitation,' Guy told him firmly. 'You'll enjoy it. Saul is bound to be there. Have you met him yet? He's head of a section of the Aarlston legal department and...'

'Yes... I was introduced to him the other day. Nice chap...'

'Have you found a house that appeals to you yet?' Guy asked him.

'Not so far. Ideally I'd like somewhere large enough for Charlotte to have her own space when she comes to stay, which means somewhere with two bedrooms and two bathrooms, but I don't really want something quite as large as a three- or four-bedroom house, from a practical point of view if nothing else.'

'Mmm...well there's a large Edwardian house on the outskirts of town which was recently converted into a series of luxury apartments, although I think most of them have already been sold. From the sound of it one of them would suit you ideally.'

'Mmm...who are the agents? It's certainly worth looking into,' Seb agreed.

The small terraced house he was currently renting was only two streets away from the one he had lived in as a child and Seb was finding staying in it faintly claustrophobic. His mother had moved away to live with her widowed sister following the death of Seb's father and Seb had no immediate family left in the town, but it seemed that everywhere he turned he was confronted with the Cooke name and the Cooke features, battalion upon battalion of assorted aunts, uncles and cousins.

And as for the Jenny Crighton supper party, that was something he would have preferred to have got out of attending but he suspected that there was no way that Guy was going to allow him to do so.

There was a certain something in Guy's voice when he mentioned Jenny Crighton's name that made Seb wonder if those rumours about Guy's feelings for Jenny before Chrissie had come into his life had been just mere rumour. Whatever the case though there was no doubt about the fact that he loved Chrissie now.

'Mmm…that looks interesting,' Olivia commented as she walked past Katie's desk and saw the estate agent's details lying there.

'Who is the prospective purchaser?' she asked curiously as she studied photographs of the elegantly shaped Edwardian rooms and the sweeping views of the grounds that surrounded the newly converted apartments.

'Me, hopefully,' Katie told her, adding ruefully, 'although the price they are asking is rather high.'

'Can't you bargain them down?' Olivia suggested practically.

Katie shook her head. 'I doubt it, there are only two apartments left.'

'Mmm…well I can see why they've sold so well, two double bedrooms, each with its own bathroom and dressing-room, a large sitting-room, dining-room and good-sized kitchen, and those views…'

'Yes, and because this one is on the top floor it's got its own balcony,' Katie told her.

'I went to view it with Dad last night and I must say that I was really impressed even if it's still an awful lot of money, but with Mum and Dad so generously offering to help me out I can just about afford it.'

'Well, you certainly won't lose out by buying it,' Olivia told her, 'not with Aarlston-Becker expanding at the rate it is and the demand for housing expanding along with them.'

'True… I see we're getting an increasing number of farming clients applying for change of use in planning permission for some of their agricultural land.'

'Yes, and there's been a lot of controversy about it

with a huge continuing debate in the local press. Those against any kind of new building on existing farmland are claiming that there are plenty of infill sites which should be used up first, while those who are in favour of granting planning permission insist the infill sites simply aren't adequate to cope with the growing demand for housing, stating that the town's prosperity is too closely linked with Aarlston to risk the threat of the company moving elsewhere because their employees can't find homes.'

'I should imagine that argument is something of a double-edged sword,' Katie murmured thoughtfully.

'Very much so,' Olivia agreed. 'The old die-hards are bitterly opposed to the Aarlston presence on the outskirts of the town claiming that it threatens its identity as a traditional market town in the centre of an agricultural area.'

'It's going to be a long-running battle, I suspect.'

After Olivia had left, Katie picked up the telephone receiver and punched in the number of the estate agents. There was no point in trying to persuade them to get the developers to drop the price of the apartment, she would just have to bite the bullet and offer the price they were asking. The apartment was, after all, perfect for her in every way, and if Olivia and her father were to be believed it would ultimately appreciate in value and prove to be a good financial investment.

While she was on the phone to the agents she decided that she would also arrange to look over the apartment again so that she could take proper measurements. Her mother had offered her some pieces of furniture she herself no longer needed including some very pretty antiques, but she would need to buy new carpets and curtains if the purchase went ahead.

*　　*　　*

Seb frowned as he studied the details of the apartment he had looked over the previous evening. On the top floor of the original Edwardian house it was one of a pair and ideally suited to his requirements. Guy had been right about that, it was exactly what he wanted even if the price was a little on the high side—not that that was a prime consideration for him—it was easily within his price range.

He had phoned Charlotte to tell her about it and she was going to travel to Haslewich from Manchester today after her classes had finished in order that she could see it. He had given her directions so that she could get a cab there and find it, and had arranged a time to meet. Afterwards he had promised to take her out for dinner.

One of the reasons Sandra had been so comfortable about accepting George's overseas posting had been because they had known that the live-in, sixth form private college where Charlotte was studying, which specialised in her chosen subjects—and where she had begged her parents to be allowed to go—placed a huge priority on its students' welfare and safety. It had been agreed that she could go, but only after a long, reassuring discussion with the school's principal about the precautions they took to supervise the students and ensure their safety. Charlotte would, also, have the benefit of members of her father's close-knit family on hand to turn to should she ever need to do so.

That of course had been before Seb himself had been headhunted by Aarlston-Becker and everything seemed to fall into place for him to be near his daughter.

Reaching for the telephone he punched in the numbers of the selling agents to confirm the appointment he had made to re-view the property this evening with Charlotte and to tell them that he was prepared to offer the full asking price.

The next stage of the purchase would involve him finding himself a solicitor and once again he suspected he would be wise to accept Guy's advice and instruct Jon Crighton to act for him.

Katie glanced at her watch. Time for her to leave if she was to meet the agent on time. Tidying up her desk she reached for her mobile phone, popping it into her bag. They were having a spell of good weather with long sunshiny days and high temperatures, which made the wearing of traditional formal office clothes too heavy and uncomfortable.

Instead, aided and abetted by her mother and her cousin, Katie had paid a visit to Chester, which she had combined with a brief but very enjoyable lunch with Luke Crighton's wife, Bobbie, and a whirlwind shopping trip that had resulted in the purchase of what she had complained to her mother was virtually a completely new wardrobe.

She had felt even more guilty about the extravagance of her purchases when her mother had insisted 'these are my treat, Katie.'

Now though, as the elegant cut of the smart black linen mix, button-back dress swirled softly round her legs, she had to admit that she was glad she had allowed herself to be persuaded. The dress was smart enough for the office without being too stuffy or formal. She had also bought a complementary jacket to go with it, and a couple of wrap skirts which could also be worn with the jacket in addition to one of several tops in matching tones.

It had been a long time since she had had any new

clothes. Although her work for the charity had not involved working at the front line, she had nevertheless been conscious of the fact that a huge discrepancy existed between her comfortably affluent Western lifestyle and those of the people they were trying to help, and besides…

She could feel the back of her throat starting to tighten with emotion. What had been the point in making herself look attractive, and allowing herself to feel womanly and sensual when she already knew that the man she wanted to be those things for would not and could not ever be hers?

Perhaps it was one of those ironic twists of their twinship that her own unrequited love for Louise's husband Gareth should echo the love Louise had once had for a married man. But then Louise had found love with Gareth and although Katie doubted that she would ever find a man to match him, she knew, too, that for her own inner peace and happiness she had to find a way of moving her life forward and of leaving that love behind.

Katie walked towards the window of her small office and stared out into the busy town square. To one side of it stood the church and running parallel to it but outside her view was a prettily elegant close of Georgian houses where her father's aunt, Ruth, lived with her American husband, Grant, whenever they were over in England.

The other three sides of the square were filled with a jumble of mixed-era buildings, Tudor wattle-and-daub cheek by jowl with Georgian town houses. The square itself had, thanks to the determination of its townspeople, retained much of its original medieval aura even if the stocks were now purely decorative and the original well had been turned into an ornamental fountain.

As young girls she and Louise used to call to see their father on their way home from school, specifically on 'pocket-money' days, hoping that he might be persuaded to add a little extra to the permitted allowance. They had giggled over the boys as they sat side by side beneath the trees on the bench donated by past worthy citizens. Together they had visited Aunt Ruth and helped her with her innovative displays of church flowers. Together they had attended regulation church services. Together they had cycled through the square to the small antique shop their mother had once half owned with Guy Cooke. Together...

As twins they had always been close, even though temperamentally they were in many ways so very different. Together they had gone to university and it had been there that they had both met Gareth Simmonds who had been one of the course lecturers.

Gareth with whom she had fallen quietly and idealistically in love...

Gareth who epitomised everything she had ever wanted in a man... Gareth who was so kind, so calm, so gentle and perceptive... Gareth who loved her sister, her twin... Gareth who could never be hers...

The view below her wavered and swam as her eyes filled with tears. Quickly she blinked them away. She had promised herself when Louise and Gareth married that she would find a way to stop loving him, that she would make herself accept him simply as her brother-in-law, as her beloved twin's husband, but every time she saw him the ache of loneliness and pain she felt at seeing the two of them so happy together was still there. She knew that Louise was hurt by her rejection of her constant invitations to go and stay with them, and she knew, too, that the gulf that was developing between the two of them disturbed her parents, especially her mother, but what could she do? What could she say? There was no way she could admit what the real problem was. And now there was the additional pain of seeing Louise with her new baby—hers and Gareth's child.

A small bitter smile twisted the softness of her mouth. Was she destined always to be wanted by men who were already committed to someone else; to always be 'second best'? She knew that Gareth would never approach her with a view to an illicit affair the way her ex-boss had done. He loved Louise far too much for that. He was so totally unaware of Katie's own anguished feelings that it seemed to her, in her present state of low self-esteem and self-respect, that it was almost as though she didn't deserve to be loved or treated well, that something about her actively encouraged men to think they could treat her badly.

No man would ever have suggested to her twin that she should have a seedy, hole-in-the-corner sexual relationship with him. No man would dream of suggesting it to any of her female cousins either, she was sure of it. Even Maddy, her brother Max's wife, who had always been regarded as the most downtrodden and to-be-pitied member of the family because of Max's appalling uncaring behaviour towards her, had turned out far stronger and determined than any of them could ever have imagined. Look at the way she had taken control of their marriage and of Max following his return home after his attack.

At last year's wedding of Bobbie's twin sister, Samantha, all the family had remarked on how much of an adoring husband and father Max had become. He was even taking on his full share of parenting following the birth of their third child, another little boy, so that

Maddy could continue with her work for the charity Aunt Ruth had originally set up. Once, the very idea of Max changing nappies and bathing babies would have been a total impossibility, but now...

So what was it about *her* that denied her the emotional happiness and support all the other Crighton women, both by birth and marriage, seemed to expect and get as their birthright? Sometimes she felt as though there was something about her that meant that she was forever condemned to live in other people's shadows...*other* people's or her twin's.

She could still remember the plans that Louise had made for them as they were growing up, plans which involved the two of them practically running the world, or at least Louise running the world; with Katie's devoted support. And Katie of course had willingly given her that support, that loyalty, that commitment, but now Louise had someone else in her life to give her those things...now Louise had the man that she, Katie, had loved and she, Katie...she, Katie had...nothing...

Outside in the square the church clock chimed the hour. Hastily Katie gathered her scattered thoughts. If she didn't leave now she was going to be late for her appointment with the selling agent.

Reaching for her jacket she headed for the door.

Half an hour later when Katie drove into the visitor's section of the apartment's car park the only other person there was a young girl who was obviously quite patiently waiting for someone. Tall and slim, wearing jeans and a cropped white top she gave Katie a warm smile as she climbed out of her car. Instinctively Katie smiled back. The girl had long dark hair and widely spaced apart warm grey eyes. For some reason Katie felt that there was something familiar about her although she had no idea what because she was certain she had never seen her before.

'Hi, I'm just waiting for my father,' the girl told Katie. 'I can see why he's decided to buy one of the apartments, Mum will love the location. I don't know where Dad is,' she added, glancing at her watch. 'He said to meet him at four-thirty. Has he telephoned you to say he's going to be late for his viewing appointment?'

As she listened to her Katie realised that the girl must have mistaken her for the viewing agent, but before she could correct her mistake the girl continued, 'I expect Dad's already told you that he works for Aarlston-Becker. He's head of their research department,' she confided with touching daughterly pride. 'I'm at a sixth form college in Manchester and we've got family in Haslewich so...

'Oh, here he is now,' she exclaimed as a large Mercedes swept round the curve of the gravel drive.

Behind it was the much smaller car driven by the estate agent which Katie recognised from her previous meeting with him, but she wasn't paying either the agent or his car any attention, instead she was concentrating on the Mercedes—and its driver. *Now* she knew why the dark hair and grey eyes the young girl had seemed so familiar. The man now stepping out of his stationary car was none other than the man who had virtually tried to run her down on her first day at work.

It was plain from his expression that he had recognised her, too, but before Katie could challenge him over his behaviour the estate agent was hurrying to join them, announcing, 'I do hope that neither of you mind but since you both want to view the properties at virtually the same time I thought we could combine the appointments.'

'*You're* buying one of the apartments?'

The words came out before Katie could silence them and she knew that her expression and tone of voice betrayed exactly what her feelings were.

The cold look she was thrown in disdainful response informed her that her dismay was more than matched by his reaction to the thought of having *her* as a neighbour, but since his daughter was flinging herself into his arms and hugging him lovingly and claiming his attention, Katie was relieved to recognise that he wasn't going to be able to respond verbally to her impetuous and betraying comment.

'Very well, if you'd like to come this way,' the estate agent suggested.

'You are interested in and are planning to purchase flat nine, Miss Crighton,' he checked as he activated the main alarm system and lock to the entrance lobby to the apartments and waited to usher them inside before continuing, 'And you are purchasing flat number ten, Mr Cooke, is that correct?'

Cooke...this man who looked nowhere near old enough to be the father of a teenage daughter was a Cooke, Katie reflected. Curiously she flicked a discreet look in his direction and then wished she hadn't as she realised that he'd caught her studying him.

She looked away as quickly as she could, but not before she had recognised that he did indeed bear the very distinctive dark and sensual Cooke good looks—the rakish and very disturbing aura of maleness and danger they all seemed to have inherited in some measure or other from their long-ago gypsy ancestor.

'In fact,' the agent continued, as he led the way to the

discreetly concealed lifts that serviced the house's upper floors, 'seeing as you are going to be close neighbours— yours are the only two apartments on the top floor— perhaps I should introduce you to one another.'

Turning to Katie and before either of them could stop him he announced, 'Miss Katie Crighton... Mr Seb Cooke...'

She was a *Crighton*, so where exactly did she fit into the extensive family tree? Seb wondered curiously as he gave Katie a narrow-eyed contemplative look. He could see at close quarters she was far prettier than he had realised that day in the street.

Her eyes were veiled now as they mirrored her body language's mute dislike of both the situation and him. Her hair, smoothly brushed instead of tousled by the breeze, hung in a thick soft wave down past her shoulders. The black dress she was wearing hinted at rather than revealed the femininity of her body.

It might not be revealing the lushly full curves of her breasts but he had a vivid memory of just how she and they had looked with the wind pressing the fabric of the top she had been wearing against their softness. In fact, unless his memory was playing tricks on him, she possessed a surprisingly voluptuous body for someone so slim.

Without realising how stern or disapproving it made him look Seb frowned. What on earth was he doing even registering the voluptuousness of an unknown young woman's body, never mind remembering it? He may not have lived totally like a monk in the years since his divorce but the demands of his work coupled with his awareness of just what an appalling husband and father he had been ensured that he kept whatever relationships he had had to discreet liaisons with women who shared his beliefs that he was simply not good marriage material.

As she saw him frown, Katie immediately felt a return of her earlier dislike of him. Heightened by her lack of self-esteem, this fuelled her inner conviction that such a sensual, rawly male man, must surely find her lacking in the kind of feminine attributes that would appeal to him. Not that she would *want* to appeal to him. Not under any circumstances.

One look at him at close quarters had confirmed that he was most definitely not her type. Too aggressive, too arrogant and far, far too sexy. Oh yes, far, *far* too sexy, because, hidden away among all the other emotional burdens she was compelling herself to carry, Katie had what she considered to be a most uncool and unappealing secret and that was...

'If you're a Crighton, can I ask... Are you one of the twin Crightons?'

As Charlotte's semi-shy but wholly warm voice broke into her thoughts, Katie focused bemusedly on her. Charlotte too, like her father, had heard all about the Crightons from Guy and Chrissie, but unlike her father she felt no self-consciousness about wanting to satisfy her curiosity about just where Katie fitted into the family jigsaw. For Charlotte, the most fascinating and interesting part of the Crighton family saga was the fact that they so regularly produced sets of twins.

'Charlotte...' Seb began warningly, but Katie shook her head. Unlike her father Charlotte was someone she had immediately felt at home with. She knew instinctively that the younger girl's question was simply a natural expression of her justifiable curiosity and so it was easy for her to smile and nod her head, explaining easily, 'Well, yes, as a matter of fact I am.'

'Does your twin live in Haslewich too? Are you and she going to share the apartment?' Charlotte pressed her.

Katie shook her head. 'No.' A small shadow crossed her face dulling her expression, a fact which Seb noticed but which Charlotte, too engrossed in waiting for her to answer and too youthfully immature to be aware of, did not.

'No, Louise my twin is married and is presently living in Brussels with... Gareth, her husband...'

Now why had she hesitated and then stumbled so awkwardly over saying her brother-in-law's name? Seb wondered thoughtfully as he caught the note of desolation in Katie's voice. Had the two women fallen out perhaps...had a rift developed between them due to the fact that their closeness had been breeched because one of them had married?

Frowning, he stood back to allow Katie and Charlotte to step into the lift ahead of him. Why on earth was he wasting time wondering about a young woman whose acquaintance he had neither the time nor the desire to pursue? Without realising what he was doing Seb let his gaze drift down to Katie's mouth. It was soft and full and oh, so infinitely kissable. He could just imagine how it would feel under his...how *she* would feel...how she would *look*, her eyes blind with a vulnerable haunted look of longing and desire that would make him want...

'Here we are... This lift is, of course, exclusively for your use and both of you will have your own passkey.'

With a start Seb dragged his thoughts back to reality.

As Katie preceded Seb into the private hallway into which both their apartments opened she was aware of feeling distinctly wobbly. What on earth was happening to her? Why had she experienced that extraordinary sensation just now, as though...as though...

Instinctively she lifted her fingers to her lips. The only man she had ever fantasised about having kissed her, the only man she wanted to have kiss her with the kind of intimacy and passion she had just been imagining was Gareth. *Gareth* and not...as her thoughts skittered to a frantic halt, refusing to allow her to question just why she had experienced that extraordinary sensation of having her mouth so expertly and intimately kissed, and by a man she neither knew nor even wanted to know, she told herself that Gareth was just about as far removed from Seb Cooke as it was possible for two men to be. Gareth was gentle, kind, reassuringly safe in his manner, while Seb Cooke was aggressive and possessed the kind of sexual aura that... Katie shuddered. What on earth would she want with such a raw, dangerous outright hunk of male sexuality...?

'This is your apartment,' the agent was saying chirpily to her, unlocking the door for her. 'As you know, you have the benefit of your own private balcony while your flat...' he turned to Seb, 'has the addition of an extra room which could be used as a third bedroom or a study.' Still smiling he crossed the hallway and unlocked the other door.

Taking advantage of Seb's preoccupation with the agent, Katie slipped inside her own apartment.

Five minutes later, having completed a closer inspection of all the rooms, she was forced to admit that she was unlikely to find anything that would suit her better. All the rooms were a good size, all the period decorative details had been retained, giving the apartment a feeling of elegance and even grandeur, and the views from the windows, which she had not really taken full account of on her previous visit, extended not just over the grounds of the house itself, all of which were there for the residents to enjoy and which were tended by a firm of gardeners, but over the surrounding countryside.

Left alone in his own apartment with Charlotte while the estate agent went to check to see if Katie had any questions she wanted to ask him, Seb turned to his daughter lifting one querying eyebrow as he asked her, 'Well...'

'It's cool,' Charlotte responded with a wide grin. 'Love the bathrooms... Yours is even big enough to have a Jacuzzi fitted if you want one.'

'*If* I want one,' Seb agreed, adding firmly, 'which I don't...'

'Dad, why *haven't* you ever re-married?' Charlotte asked him seriously now.

While Seb was frowningly wondering how best to answer her, she continued a little uncertainly,

'It isn't because of me is it... I mean I know that...well Mum never really said much about...about things, but I did once overhear her talking to George about it and she said that having me had been the final straw for you...'

Seb studied her downcast head wondering what on earth he could say. As close as they had grown the subject of his marriage to her mother and their subsequent divorce was not one they had ever discussed, and man-like he had always been reluctant to raise a subject which, he was forced to admit, did not reflect well on himself.

'I rather think what your mother was trying to say was that my adolescent and totally selfish reaction to the demands a baby made on her time and our marriage were the last straw for *her*,' Seb corrected Charlotte gently.

'The reason our marriage didn't survive was wholly and totally down to me, Charlotte... I was a selfish wretch, and far too immature when we got married to think about anyone other than myself. Your mother and I met at university, fell into what we believed was love but what, with a bit of perspective, I think we both soon realised was really only lust, married...and...and then you came along and you have no idea how much I regret the years I've lost with you and my own unforgivable selfishness...'

'M-Mum did say once that had the pair of you been older or a bit more worldly-wise, you'd both have known that what you had together was wonderful for an intense and passionate affair, but not for marriage. She said, too, that while *she* was the one who initiated things between the two of you, you were the one with the old-fashioned moral principles who insisted that you should get married—if you were going to have sex.'

Seb grimaced. What Charlotte had just said was quite true. Eighteen months his senior, Sandra had had other boyfriends, other relationships, before she had met him—neither of them had come to their own affair as novice lovers. But with his own upbringing, his knowledge of what could happen in the aftermath of a passionate relationship for the woman who was left on her own, seen first-hand through the history of his own family—Cooke men had a certain notorious reputation for their alleged propensity to father children outside wedlock—he had felt it necessary to prove that he was different, above the kind of much criticised behaviour his name had branded him with. Perhaps his insistence on marrying Sandra had been a righteous and ridiculous piece of over-reaction, but if he was honest with himself

Seb knew that, given the same situation again, he would probably have reacted in exactly the same way.

His father had always been a stern critic of the haphazard morals of some members of the Cooke clan. As a boy growing up, Seb could remember that there had been tight-lipped conversations between his parents about the sudden arrival of a new and unexpected member of the family who did not always carry his or her father's name. Both of his parents had been insistent that that was a family inheritance of which they most certainly did not approve. And nor, no more so, did Seb.

Seb was brought back to the present as Charlotte squeezed his arm lovingly and kissed his cheek.

'I'm glad we've had this little talk,' she told him almost maternally. 'And I wish that you could find someone nice to marry Dad... I liked Katie Crighton, didn't you?'

Seb frowned as she looked at him, but Charlotte only returned his look with one of filial innocence and before Seb could warn her that even if he had been looking for someone, Katie Crighton was most definitely not his type, the estate agent had returned.

Ten minutes later as Seb drove out of the house's grounds behind Katie and the estate agent, he made a mental note to get in touch with Jon Crighton and set the wheels in motion for the purchase of the apartment. Now that he had decided to buy and had had his offer accepted, he wanted to get the formalities over and done with as soon as possible so that he could move in.

As she drove out of the house's grounds ahead of Seb Cooke, Katie was wishing that she might have had someone else, anyone else, but him, for her new and nearest neighbour. Not that she was likely to see much of him she acknowledged, on two counts. According to what Charlotte had told her she could guess that his job would be very demanding and from the way he had looked at her she had seen that he was as pleased about having her for a neighbour as she was him. What was his wife like? she wondered. Very glamorous and sexy no doubt. He was that kind of man—you could see at a glance. He just exuded sexuality... Not like Gareth. Gareth was a man for snuggling up to in front of a lovely log fire... Gareth was a comfort and reassurance, safe and...

And there was no way that anyone, any woman, would ever describe Seb Cooke as any of those things, but most especially safe. Why, you only had to think about his family's reputation. There was a smouldering sexual energy about him that rubbed her up the wrong way and brought all of her own antagonism towards him out making her feel prickly and on her guard, wary and filled with unfamiliarly strong emotions.

Even the way he had looked at her. Katie tensed as she tried to banish the unwanted memory of that startling reaction she had experienced when she had almost felt as though she could sense the heat of his breath, his *mouth* on hers. It had been a mistake, an accident, a ridiculous fluke caused by heaven alone knew what mix up of signals inside her body. No doubt Seb himself would have an explanation for such awareness. He, after all, was the research scientist and no doubt fully *au fait* with the confusing mixture of chemicals and in-built programming which were responsible for what less rational people called 'emotions.'

To her relief as she looked in her driving mirror she saw that they were going in opposite directions to their different destinations as she indicated to turn left to drive home to her parents' house.

CHAPTER THREE

'Mmm... What a wonderful smell,' Katie enthused as she walked into the kitchen where her mother was busy cooking. Originally a farmer's daughter from Cheshire, Jenny Crighton had the kind of homemaking skills that at one stage of her young married life had made her feel very dull and old-fashioned. Who wanted a wife who could grow, preserve and cook her own fruit and vegetables in an era which had fallen in love with Twiggy look-alikes; fragile, big-eyed dolly birds? Who wanted a wife with a healthy build, thick curly hair and freckles when the fashion was for chalk-white pallor and long straight locks?

It had taken a long time for her to learn that Jon Crighton, her husband, loved her very deeply, but these last few years since the birthday party thrown to celebrate her husband's and his twin brother's half century, had seen a renaissance in their marriage and had brought her more joy and happiness than she had once believed she could ever have—and it showed. She still had the trim feminine figure of her youth, but as a young girl she had been self-effacing, a little awkward and shy, now she had a mature self-confidence that came not just from knowing how much her husband loved her nor even from being the pivot of her busy family household, but from feeling at ease with herself.

'It's for supper tonight. You haven't forgotten that we're having an informal party have you?'

Katie gave her an apologetic look.

'Oh heavens, yes I had,' she admitted, adding by way of explanation, 'It's been such a frantic week, what with my own conveyance and then Olivia having to take extra time off.'

'Mmm... Well at least the doctor has confirmed the fever and temperature is only a childhood upset and not meningitis as Olivia first feared. You will be joining us this evening though, won't you?'

'Mmm... What time are you expecting people?'

'In about an hour,' her mother told her.

'Right, I'll go up and have a shower and get changed and then I'll come down and give you a hand. Is Dad back?' she asked as she helped herself to one of the too-tempting and still-warm fruit buns her mother had just put onto a wire rack to cool.

'Yes...just... That will give you indigestion,' she warned Katie with a mock serious look as she tapped her hand.

'Oh, and by the way, I rang Louise this morning...'

Katie, who had been about to go upstairs, tensed, her heart starting to thud unevenly. Every mention of her twin reminded her of Gareth and brought home to her the emptiness of her own life in contrast to the love that filled Louise's.

'You know we're having a special party for your grandfather soon,' her mother was continuing. 'Well, both Maddy and I think that we ought to have as many from the family there as possible. Having the family around him means so much to Ben and he's getting so frail...'

Katie's eyebrows rose.

'The family means so much, does it? Well he certainly doesn't *show* it,' she told her mother dryly. 'With the exception of Max and of course uncle David, I get the impression that he doesn't care that much for anyone.'

'Oh, that's just his way,' Jenny assured her sunnily. 'You wouldn't believe how proud he is of all of you.'

'No, I wouldn't,' Katie agreed wryly. 'He told me when he learned that Lou and I were going to study law that women and the law simply didn't mix, and that women were far too emotional to make good lawyers...'

'He *is* a bit old-fashioned,' her mother acknowledged, 'and since David left...' She paused and sighed.

'Do you think Uncle David *will* ever come back?' Katie asked her mother curiously. 'I mean, to just disappear like that... I know that Olivia makes no real secret of the fact that she doesn't want him to come back, but Jack...'

She paused and frowned as both she and her mother remembered how, when Louise had first moved to Brussels to work, Jack and their brother Joss had illicitly taken time off school to go and search for Jack's missing father. And then later, undeterred by Louise's father's decision that his twin brother should be allowed to make his own decisions as to whether or not to be reunited with his family, Jack had secretly made arrangements to fly out to Jamaica on the same plane as Jon's eldest son, Max.

Max had callously played on his grandfather's love for him and for his son, David, on what was to have been, for Max, an all-expenses-paid luxury holiday and an escape from his wife and a difficult situation professionally, all cloaked in the disguise of wanting to look for David at Ben's behest.

The ensuing near tragedy had resulted, not just in Max's total transformation and metamorphosis, but also in a much deeper and adult understanding between Jack and his Uncle Jon, but all the family knew that a small part of Jack would also always be scarred by his father's disappearance and his apparent rejection of him, no matter how much love and reassurance he received from Jon and Jenny.

'I don't know if David will ever come back,' her mother admitted now. 'We don't even know where he is. For Ben's sake…' She paused and bit her lip but Katie knew what she was thinking.

'Grandfather *is* getting very frail,' she agreed quietly. 'If Uncle David is going to come back I hope he doesn't leave it too long…or until it's too late…'

'It wouldn't be easy for David to come back and I'm not sure he actually possesses the courage he would need to do so…' Jenny replied.

'Mmm… He and Max were very alike, weren't they?' Katie acknowledged. 'But Max has changed and so…'

'Max *has* changed,' her mother agreed. 'He and Maddy will be here this evening, by the way. Maddy did say she wanted to have a word with you. They're hoping to buy another house for the mums and babes and I suspect she's going to ask you if you'd do all the legal work for them.'

The family charity originally begun by Ben Crighton's sister, Ruth, had grown from a single house with individual rooms for young single mothers, into an organisation which now provided homes for single parents of both sexes as well as their young children, and which was constantly having to find more accommodation for its protégé's parents.

One of Maddy's contributions had been the development of a scheme which allowed the young parents to train for jobs and then to go out to work while their children were looked after safely at an in-house crèche.

And not all of their single parents were female. They now had a small group of young men who, for one reason or another, were the sole parents to their children.

It was a very worthwhile cause and one which all the Crighton women both supported and were involved in to some extent or another. Katie and Louise had both worked voluntarily with the scheme during their university breaks and Katie was not surprised to hear that Maddy, as the charity's main working executive, was in the process of obtaining further housing.

'Who else is coming?' she asked her mother as she scooped up the last few crumbs of her pilfered cake.

'Mmm… Olivia and Caspar, Tullah and Saul and a handful of other people. Oh, and Chrissie and Guy…'

'Guy Cooke?' Katie enquired so sharply that her mother frowned.

'Yes. Why?'

A long, long time ago, or so it seemed now to Jenny, Guy had made it plain to her that if she had a neglectful husband then she most certainly had a very appreciative business partner and one who, given the opportunity, would like to put their relationship on a much closer intimate footing.

But that had been before she and Jon had sorted out their problems and before Guy had met Chrissie, and so far as Jenny knew, there was now no reason whatsoever for Katie to have *that* particular note of reservation in her voice when she repeated Guy's name, and certainly none for her unexpected emphasis on the Cooke part of Guy's name.

Katie, of both her girls, was the one to whom Jenny felt the closest, the one who was most like her in temperament and yet, conversely, Katie was also the one who was the least forthcoming, the least given to confidence.

For a long time Jenny had been concerned about her daughter, knowing with maternal instinct that she wasn't happy, but Katie had never been the kind of person you could coax or persuade into discussing anything she did not want to discuss. Jenny had her own ideas and thoughts about what was making her so unhappy and if she was right...

Katie had always tended to idealise people, to put them on a small pedestal, to invest them with virtues of her own making. She had a far gentler and more romantic nature than Louise, her twin, a far less robust attitude towards life—and men.

And now as she looked at her withdrawn expression, Jenny decided that it might not be a good moment to tell her that she had invited Guy to bring another Cooke along to her supper party with him.

Jenny had not yet met Seb Cooke, but she had heard all about him from both Guy and Chrissie. Naturally maternal and warm-hearted as well as being a generous hostess, Jenny had immediately suggested to them both that they should bring Seb with them when they came over to supper. From what Guy had told her about him it sounded as though, despite all his family connections in the town, he might be feeling a little isolated.

'He isn't the easiest of people to get to know,' Guy had warned her. 'In fact, some folk find him a little bit off-putting and intimidating. He's a scientist, of course, and very analytical, and like me he's known the burden of being a Cooke who doesn't fit into the normal and expected male Cooke mould.'

As Katie went upstairs to change and prepare for the evening she was frowning. Her father had asked her if she would take over one of his few remaining conveyancing cases, explaining that what was to have been a simple court case had developed into something much more complicated, meaning that he couldn't do the work as quickly as their new client wished.

'Nice chap. You'll like him,' he had told Katie with a smile. 'Seb Cooke... He...'

'Seb Cooke! You want me to act for *him*?'

Her father had raised an eyebrow when he had heard the antagonism in her voice.

'What's wrong? I thought...'

'Nothing's wrong...' Katie had fibbed. The situation and her own feelings were far too complicated and personal to be explained to her father. How could she tell him that the main reason she disliked Seb so much was because of his intense sexuality...that something about him, about his power as a man, made her all the more aware of her own incompleteness as a woman.

'He's buying the apartment adjacent to mine,' was all she could allow herself to say.

'Yes, I know,' her father agreed, and then wisely decided not to pursue the subject.

Katie had changed since she had reached maturity. Something had happened to her, hurt her, and much as he longed to help, he felt that it was impossible for him to pry. She was an adult now and if she wouldn't even confide in her mother then who was he, a mere man—a mere *father*—to push for confidences she quite plainly did not want to share.

Her father had an appointment with Seb on Monday, an appointment *she* would now have to keep in his place. Fortunately most of the work had already been done and it was simply a matter of Seb signing some forms and then, hopefully, at the end of the week when completion for the sale would take place, that would be an end of the matter. He would still be her neighbour of course, but there she would be able to keep her distance.

What kind of man was he anyway? she fumed a few minutes later as she stood under the warm lash of the shower. He was buying the apartment in his own name and not putting it into the joint names of himself and his wife. That old-fashioned kind of chauvinism was something she detested and fortunately was rare now. The majority of men accepted that their wives, their partners, *were* equal to them in every way and behaved financially accordingly.

She might, Katie conceded, be a little old-fashioned when it came to matters of personal intimacy, but she was thoroughly modern in outlook when it came to matters of equality between the two sexes, whether that equality related to financial aspects of a relationship or the emotional and physical ones, and so far as she was concerned, a man who was selfish towards his partner financially, who refused to accept that she had absolute parity with him, was just as likely to be selfish both emotionally and physically.

Max, her elder brother, had once been that type of man and she had seen at uncomfortably close quarters just how destructive an effect that had had on his marriage. What was Seb Cooke's wife like? Katie wondered curiously. Attractive? Very, she suspected. Seb had struck her as the type of man who would, as an arrogant right, demand perfection in every aspect of his life, and then there was the stunningly attractive daughter as living proof of her parents' good looks.

Was this wife clever, witty…fun to be with? Did those steel-grey eyes glow with warmth and passion when their glance rested on her?

Katie gave herself a small mental warning shake. If she wasn't careful she was going to turn into the kind of sad person who, without an emotional focus of her own in her life, worried incessantly and even perhaps a little obsessively, about the flaws of people who were at best mere acquaintances. And that was behaviour that was…what? Typical of what, one hundred and fifty years ago, might have been the ways of the unmarried, and therefore supposedly the unwanted daughter of the family who remained at home to look after her ageing parents.

Well, her own parents were far from ageing and she was living in a time when it was publicly documented that the women who enjoyed the best health and the least stress both physically and mentally, were those who had elected to remain independent—who had *chosen* to remain independent, Katie reminded herself inwardly, not those who were forced to confront the unhappy knowledge that they loved a man who did not return that love, and had no option other than to remain alone.

Perhaps it was inevitable in a way that both she and Louise *should* love the same man since they were twins…but Bobbie and Sam were twins and Bobbie loved Luke and Sam loved Liam.

But then there were certain personal similarities between those two men, both in looks and in character, and there was only one Gareth, could only ever be one Gareth.

Outside the sun was still shining. It was a lovely warm evening and Katie knew from past experience that her parents' guests would spill out of the house to explore and enjoy the gardens, so she opened her wardrobe door and looked for something appropriate to wear.

The soft chambray skirt she decided upon was both

practical and pretty and with it she put on a white cap-sleeve T-shirt which had been a present from Louise.

'It's too tight and too...'

'...sexy,' Louise had teased her, her eyes sparkling with amusement. 'It's meant to be. It suits you, Katie. Since you've been working for that charity you've started wearing things that are far too dowdy and matronly for you. You've got a gorgeous body...much better than mine... Oh, yes you have,' she had insisted before Katie had been able to protest that the last thing she wanted to look was 'sexy,' but then Louise had unwittingly touched a nerve when she had added teasingly,

'Gareth commented the last time he saw you that Ma dresses more stylishly than you do. I know how you feel about ostentatious consumerism when other people are having to do without, but there's no reason why you shouldn't wear inexpensive clothes that flatter you instead of opting for ones that don't. And don't forget,' she had added winningly, 'every time you buy something you're helping *other* people to earn...'

Remembering the seriousness of her twin's voice as she delivered this piece of wisdom made Katie smile as she slipped on the pretty delicate gold earrings which had been Louise and Gareth's Christmas present to her. They matched the gold bangle they had given her when she had been their bridesmaid.

Arriving downstairs five minutes later, Katie shooed her mother out of the kitchen so that she too could shower and get ready for her guests, reminding her, 'Ma...don't worry, I'll finish off everything down here...'

'Would you? Oh, and Katie, could you do something

with the flowers I've put in the laundry room. You really have inherited Aunt Ruth's talent with them.'

'Mmm…and I wonder which ancestor *you* inherited your silver tongue from,' Katie teased her mother as she obligingly headed for the laundry room and the flowers.

CHAPTER FOUR

'YOU'LL like Jenny and Jon,' Chrissie told Seb warmly after they had picked him up from the house he was renting, adding ruefully, 'Oh, but I'd forgotten you'll have met Jon already, won't you, since he's handling the legal side of your property purchase.'

'As a matter-of-fact I haven't,' Seb informed her. 'I've got an appointment on Monday to sign my contract, but it seems that he's going to be tied up in court so his daughter will be dealing with it.'

'His daughter...' Guy frowned and then smiled. 'Of course I'd forgotten that Katie was working with Jon and Olivia now.'

'Katie... Katie Crighton?' Seb questioned him sharply so that both Chrissie and Guy exchanged automatic close-couple looks before Guy turned to Seb and asked him,

'Yes, do you know her?'

'We've met,' Seb told him brusquely. Then, sensing their mutual curiosity, informed them drily, 'As it happens she's buying the apartment next to mine.'

'Oh really,' Chrissie looked interested. 'Jenny did say when I last spoke to her that Katie was looking for somewhere local. It's such a shame about her having to leave the charity. She was really enjoying working for them.'

'Of the two of them, she always was more intensely caring in that sort of way,' Guy informed Seb. 'I can remember how when they were children, both of them were involved in sponsoring African orphans, but it was

Katie who not only gave her spending money but came down to the shop and insisted on spending all her spare time polishing the furniture to earn extra money for them.'

'Well I suppose there is bound to be an element of competition between them,' Seb commented briefly and with what Guy felt was an unfamiliar and an uncharacteristic note of censure in his voice. Then, before he could correct Seb's misapprehension and inform him that in fact Katie had insisted on quietly and discreetly sharing the earnings with her twin so that their shared contributions were ultimately 'equal,' Chrissie was asking Seb if he remembered the family from his own childhood in the town.

'Obviously I know the name,' Seb confirmed, adding cynically, 'After all, it's almost as synonymous with Haslewich as the name Cooke, although for a very different reason. From what I can remember, old man Crighton was considered to be very much among the great and good of the area, a very traditional *pater familiae*... I do once remember going to a children's party up at Queensmead but it was quite definitely an "us and them" affair, the rich distributing alms to the poor sort of thing...'

'Mmm... I remember those days,' Guy confirmed. 'But things are completely different now. Jon is as different from his father as chalk is from cheese and the current young adult generation of Crightons are a lively multi-talented bunch whose company I'm sure you'll enjoy.'

Seb forbore to inform his cousin that his two previous encounters with Katie Crighton did not incline him to share his optimism.

He had not exactly been enthusiastic about the eve-

ning to start with and had he known just who Katie
Crighton was he would've made every effort to exclude
himself from the event. Now, of course, it was too late.

He started to frown as he had a sharp mental picture
of Katie the first time he had seen her. Seb felt his stomach muscles tighten in protest at the feelings *that* memory evoked. At thirty-eight he considered himself, if not
exactly past being sexually aware of and aroused by the
sight and thought of a pretty woman, then certainly well
able to control the physical effects of such thoughts. But
now, as then, his body was proving him wrong.

Irritably he tried to deny the impact of his visual memory of her as Guy drove in through the gates to Jon and
Jenny's comfortable home.

The heady summer warmth of the evening had prompted
Jenny to organise a buffet table under the trees in their
pretty orchard and as Seb followed Guy and Chrissie in
under the rose and honeysuckle hedge which separated
the orchard from the rest of the garden, the first person
he saw was Katie.

She had her back to him and was standing beside Saul
Crighton, who Seb recognised from work, pouring him
a glass of what Seb later discovered was her mother's
special and highly potent strawberry wine cooler. The
scene in front of him couldn't have been more idyllic,
Seb recognised. The meadow grass was sprinkled with
wild flowers, the breeze was scented with roses and the
still warm air hummed with harmonious happy voices.
Even a half-dozen or so young children who were playing together in one corner of the orchard seemed to be
sharing one another's company rather than squabbling
noisily or quarrelling.

As Seb watched, one of the slightly older girls detached herself from the group and walked over to Saul Crighton leaning against him whilst he wrapped his arm tenderly around her.

As Seb looked on Katie reached out and brushed a stray lock of hair out of the girl's eyes. Quickly Seb turned away. The small scene being enacted in front of him reminded him of his own loss as a father. When he looked back now it appalled him that he could ever have behaved so selfishly and how it hurt to recognise how much he had missed.

'Come on, let me introduce you to Jenny and Jon,' Guy was saying, touching him on his arm and directing him towards the older couple standing a few feet away.

Five minutes later he was forced to admit that Guy had been right when he had told him he would like Jenny and Jon Crighton as Jenny in particular possessed a warmth which was extremely attractive and welcoming. And before he knew what he was doing Seb found that he was confiding to Jenny that one of the main reasons he had moved back to the area was so that he could be close to Charlotte.

'During the early years of Charlotte's life I was guilty of being an absent father,' he heard himself telling Jenny ruefully. 'I've been very fortunate in that Charlotte has forgiven me, and *she* has been very fortunate in that my ex-wife's second husband and her stepfather has given her the love and security I failed to provide.'

'We all mature at different stages,' Jenny responded gently. 'You must have been very young yourself when your daughter was born.'

Several yards away on the other side of the orchard Katie was just about to pour a glass of cooler for Saul's wife Tullah when Tullah enquired in an admiring whisper,

'Who on earth is that with your mother?'

As Katie turned round to look, her eyes widened in disbelief and dismay.

'He's…it's Seb Cooke,' she told Tullah curtly.

'You've met him?' Tullah questioned, her eyebrows lifting a little as she readily interpreted the dismay in Katie's voice and expression.

'Briefly,' Katie admitted reluctantly, and then knowing that it was bound to become common family knowledge, she added even more reluctantly, 'He's buying the apartment next to mine…'

'He is? *Wow*! Lucky *you*…' Tullah sighed mock-enviously while Saul raised his own eyebrows and questioned teasingly, 'What's this?'

'No one for you to worry about,' Tullah quickly reassured him, linking her arm with his and snuggling up to his side. 'But he is gorgeous and now that you've told me who he is I can see his likeness to Guy.'

'Mmm…he's already caused quite a flutter in the research labs,' Saul admitted. 'I think some of the girls are running a book on who will be the first to have a date with him.'

'He's a married man,' Katie protested stiffly, looking disapproving.

'You mean he was a married man,' Saul corrected her. 'According to the Aarlston-Becker grape-vine he is very much divorced and has been for a considerable length of time.'

Seb Cooke was *divorced*. For some inexplicable reason Katie discovered that her legs had gone oddly weak and that she wanted to sit down. Quite why the discovery that the elegant wife she had visualised for Seb did not actually exist should have such a dramatic physical effect on her she had no idea and nor did she wish to have, she warned herself hastily as her thoughts threatened to go into overdrive.

'Why don't you go and offer him a drink?' Tullah suggested giving Katie a sparkling-eyed look.

'I'm sure if he wants one he'll come over and ask...besides I've just remembered, there's something I've left in the oven,' Katie fibbed, pink-cheeked, as she hastily thrust the jug into Tullah's hand and started to hurry back to the house making sure as she did so that she took a circuitous route through the orchard that would keep her as far away from Seb as possible.

Unfortunately though, her father had seen her and remembering that he had asked her to handle Seb's conveyancing, he called her over.

Reluctantly Katie abandoned her flight and walked warily towards the small group which included her parents and Guy and Chrissie as well as Seb.

'Katie, I was just explaining to Seb here that you are going to be handling his conveyance,' her father told her calmly as she reached them.

'Your daughter and I have already met,' Seb informed Jon formally as her father prepared to make the introductions.

As she responded to Seb's unsmiling greeting, Katie wondered if anyone else other than herself had noticed his distancing reference to her as 'your daughter'.

'It's quite a coincidence the two of you buying adjoining apartments,' Chrissie Cooke commented lightly.

Seb gave a small shrug before responding,

'They're ideal for anyone living alone who wants the space and privacy they afford. The size of their rooms is an asset together with no maintenance of the beautiful gardens.'

'Mmm... I believe the builders have even renovated the tennis courts so that the residents will be able to use them,' Chrissie enthused.

'Do you play tennis, Seb,' Jenny asked conversationally.

'I used to,' Seb acknowledged. 'Although...'

'Katie plays,' Chrissie chimed in.

Hot-cheeked, Katie denied quickly, 'Not any more... I don't really have time, and since Louise got married...'

'Louise is Katie's twin,' Chrissie explained to Seb. 'She and her husband are living in Brussels at the moment.

'When are they next coming over, Jenny?' she asked Katie's mother.

'We're hoping to arrange a family party for Ben soon,' Jenny responded, turning to Seb to tell him, 'Ben, my father-in-law, hasn't been in very good health for quite some time. This celebration isn't for a particular reason other than the fact he likes to get to see all the children. As much as he pretends his grandchildren and family irritate him, privately he would be dreadfully hurt if they didn't all come to see him every once in a while.'

'I suppose he *does* love us in his way,' Katie agreed, momentarily forgetting her discomfort at seeing Seb. 'But it's Uncle David he really wants...'

'David is my husband's brother,' Jenny explained quietly to Seb.

'Did I hear you mention my father's name?' Olivia Crighton suddenly chimed in on the point of walking past with her husband Caspar, but instead coming over to join them as she heard them discussing David.

'The family's black sheep.'

Seb frowned a little as he heard the challenging bitterness and dislike in her voice and noticed that it was
Jon who moved over to her taking hold of her hand and
patting it almost paternally as he soothed her, 'We were
just saying how close he and Dad always were Livvy...'

'Don't remind me,' Olivia responded, refusing to be
mollified. 'If Gramps hadn't spoiled him so much...' She
stopped and shook her head, apologising to Jenny, 'I'm
sorry, but gramps was criticising me the other day for
continuing to work even though I've got the children...'

'He can be very difficult, I know,' Jenny agreed, turning to Katie and suggesting, 'Katie, why don't you take
Guy, Chrissie and Seb up to the house so they can get
themselves something to eat. I like to make sure my
victims are well fed and slothful before I go on the attack,' Jenny told Seb beguilingly with a warm smile.

'Go on the attack?' Seb couldn't resist questioning as
Katie started to lead the way back to the house.

'Mmm...' Guy began to explain, but Katie beat him
to it telling Seb protectively,

'My mother is a very caring person. She works very
hard to raise funds to help support and maintain a local
charity which was originally founded by my father's
Aunt Ruth.'

'Mother and Baby homes,' Chrissie told Seb enthusiastically. 'We all do what we can to help but Jenny
and Maddy between them carry the heaviest responsibility for everything.'

'Thanks in the main to Saul, Aarlston-Becker already
underwrites a special fun day for the children, which is
held annually. That's due to come up quite soon, isn't
it, Katie?' Chrissie asked her.

'Mmm... Aarlston combined it with a group day off

which means that nearly all the staff are also involved in the event.'

'Yes, it's held in the grounds of Fitzburgh Place and I warn you now, Seb,' Guy teased, 'you can fully expect to be roped in.'

'Guy organises the marquees and the entertainers as his contribution,' Chrissie informed Seb.

Guy gave a modest shrug.

'It's nothing really. What we normally do is arrange the event to tie in with one that we're giving commercially up at the Hall so that we can give the kids their day out either for free or at a minimum cost. Lord Astlegh allows us to use the parkland for free and you'd be amazed at the amount of talent there is among Aarlston employees.'

'...and among your family,' Chrissie reminded him. 'Last year's fortune-teller was a really big hit. Who was she? You never would tell me...'

'No, and I'm not going to now,' Guy informed her. 'Her identity is a professional secret.'

'Mmm...well, she was definitely a Cooke,' Chrissie murmured.

'Well, of course. What else would you expect with our gypsy genes?' Guy countered teasingly.

They had reached the house and as Katie led the way into the large conservatory off the kitchen where the main buffet table had been laid out she decided that now that her duty was done she could safely escape. Seb's brooding presence was having a decidedly disturbing effect on her senses. Was that really his aftershave she could smell and was so acutely aware of, that potently musky odour?

As they started to help themselves to the buffet another group came in including Saul and Tullah and their children. Almost immediately Saul and Seb began to discuss some mutually interesting aspect of their work at Aarlston-Becker but for some reason, instead of retreating back into the garden, Katie discovered that she was simply staying where she was listening and observing.

Saul said something which made Seb laugh. It was the first time Katie had seen him properly relaxed and a warning feathering of an emotion she didn't want to name curled dangerously down her spine. She wasn't attracted to him she told herself fiercely, she couldn't possibly be, she loved Gareth.

Saul's daughter Meg tugged on her father's sleeve and Katie saw quite plainly the look of sombre reflection that darkened Seb's eyes as he watched Saul turn to respond to his daughter.

He envied Saul. But why? Katie had recognised immediately when she had seen him with Charlotte just how close and loving a bond there was between the two of them.

As though she had guessed what was going through Katie's mind, Chrissie who had been standing beside her and who had also observed the small bit of byplay, explained in a quiet voice, 'Seb feels very guilty about the fact that he was an absent father for much of the time when Charlotte was young.'

'He *abandoned* his wife and child?' Katie demanded sharply.

She had turned her back towards Seb to speak with Chrissie and was therefore unaware of the fact that he had both disengaged himself from his conversation with Saul and overheard her own sharp question until he spoke from immediately behind her, his voice bitingly harsh as he told her quietly,

'No, I did not *abandon* them...'

Katie felt her face start to burn as Chrissie discreetly melted away leaving her to confront Seb on her own.

Katie knew that by rights she ought to apologise, if only because Seb was a guest in her parents' home, but for some extraordinary reason, a streak of wilful stubbornness normally more likely to manifest itself in her twin than in her, suddenly propelled her into defensive action, causing her to walk angrily towards the door at the same time throwing acidly over her shoulder,

'But you did *leave* them, *desert* them...'

As she walked into the narrow passage which linked the conservatory to the laundry room through which she had intended to make her escape, to her consternation Seb followed her, pulling the door to behind him, his height and breadth of shoulder taking up so much of the narrow space that as she turned to face him, Katie felt almost as though she was actually being deprived of air to breathe.

'Why you...!'

Katie's eyes widened as she saw how very angry Seb was, a dark flush burning along his cheek bones, his eyes the colour of molten metal. A sharp frisson of fear ran through her body, but she refused to give in to it or to be intimidated by it, or by him. Stubbornly she stood her ground.

His close proximity to her in the passage though was making her feel acutely claustrophobic. She had always had a fear of small enclosed spaces, something to do perhaps with the fact that once as a young child she had become trapped in a cupboard, but as she turned intending to walk away, she froze with shock as Seb suddenly reached for her, taking hold of her upper arm to restrain her as he told her furiously, 'Oh no you don't.... *What* gives you the right to sit in judgement of me?' he demanded curtly. 'Have you ever been married? Have you ever had a child? No, of course you haven't, you're...'

You're one of fortune's favourites he had been about to tell her. You're cushioned and protected from the realities of life by your parents and your background, but when he saw the white, tight look that drove the colour from her face and felt the way she froze, tensing her body almost as though he had physically hurt her, he stopped while his scientist's analytical brain tried to process all the conflicting information he was receiving.

Katie stared at him. *How* had he guessed her increasingly humiliating secret? She could feel her heart racing, her body taut with anxiety. He couldn't possibly have actually guessed how she really felt, could he?

From the moment Gareth and Louise had announced their love for one another Katie had made a fierce promise to herself that she would somehow find a way of making a fulfilling life for herself without Gareth in it. And she had worked hard and determinedly towards this goal.

She had a career that she found very challenging and fulfilling, a family and friends who she truly loved and who she knew truly loved her in return. And she was determined that she would never ever allow her love for Gareth to turn to bitterness or envy over her twin's happiness. But at the same time, deep down inside, she knew there was a part of her that suffered, not just a sense of loss but a sense of insecurity as well over the fact that she had not experienced the kind of sexual fulfilment she had often heard her peers discussing.

She had tried to reassure herself that there was nothing to be ashamed of in feeling not just a little enviously curious about how it must feel to share true sexual intimacy with a lover, but also a little anxious about the fact that because of her love for Gareth she had allowed herself to become isolated on her own small personal island of inexperience and inhibition.

Of course, the thought of sex for sex's sake was naturally totally repugnant to her, but she couldn't help wishing sometimes that way back before she had met and fallen for Gareth she could have known the rite of passage that would have meant that she did not now have that irritating gap in her life's experience, that worrying chink of insecurity in her female armour.

And certainly the last thing she wanted now was to have Seb Cooke finding that chink and taunting her for it.

Pulling away from him she demanded sharply,

'Let go of me...'

Let go of her... Seb hadn't even realised he was still holding her arm, but once he did...once she had drawn his attention to the fact that she was virtually his prisoner, she who had dared to accuse him...to criticise and condemn him...

The passageway wasn't very well lit by its single solitary small window, but there was more than enough light coming in through it for Seb to see the shocked disbelieving expression widen Katie's eyes as he closed the distance between them and tightened his grip on her arm.

'Stop it...*what* are you doing?' Katie protested frantically as she felt the hard heat of his body pressing hers against the passage wall, one hand on her shoulder, the other on her waist as he held her pinned there.

There wasn't time for her to feel frightened or to do anything more to try to express her outrage as he bent his head and covered her half-open mouth with his own.

Thanks to the unwanted attentions of her ex-boss

Katie knew exactly how it felt to have a man kiss her against her will, but the sensations, the emotions, that coursed through her body as *Seb* kissed her bore no resemblance whatsoever to those she had experienced then.

Dizzily she wondered where they were and why in their place she was experiencing this odd feeling of lightheadedness; why she was hearing this deafening, thudding rushing sound that reminded her of breaking surf, pounding on a beach. She recognised it was, in actual fact, the roar of her pulse combined with the frantic surge of her heartbeat and she wondered, too, why her mouth seemed to be actually enjoying the sensation of the hard warmth of Seb's expertly caressing it, but before she could answer any of these questions, her brain went into overload, short circuiting its own ability to reason or analyse *any* of what was happening.... Her eyelashes fluttered, her body softened, her hand lifted to touch Seb's face as a small sound of sensual pleasure purred in her throat.

Seb lifted his hand from Katie's waist to the temptingly soft curve of her breast. Through her top and her bra he could feel the delicate pout of her nipple. Desire kicked through him in a shocking breath-stopping surge. Against his hand Katie's nipple hardened provocatively.

As Seb's body read her responsiveness to him it reacted instinctively and Katie's sensually soft purr gave way to a shocked strangled gasp as she felt the betraying hardness of Seb's body.

Outside, behind the closed door, one of the children called Katie's name. As Seb heard it, it brought him back to reality. Immediately he lifted his body away from Katie's releasing her and just as immediately Katie pushed herself away from him and darted down the passage.

The hallway was empty—thankfully—and Katie headed instinctively for the stairs and the sanctuary of her bedroom.

From outside in the garden she could hear the laughter and chatter of her parents' guests but *she* felt as remote from them as though she were on another planet, their voices nothing more than a backdrop to the appalled anguish of her own thoughts. Her whole body was trembling, shuddering from head to foot, galvanised by what she told herself was her total revulsion for what had happened.

The way Seb Cooke had treated her, *touched* her, was unforgivable…*unforgettable*…an insult…an *assault* against both her emotions and her most dearly held moral beliefs. She hadn't *encouraged* him, she hadn't *wanted* him.

Hot-faced she closed her eyes, choking back the devastatingly honest inner voice that told her that she wasn't being truthful with herself.

Squeezing her eyes tightly closed Katie whispered under her breath, 'All right, so I did…react to him, but that was just *physical*…*any* man could have…' Biting her lip she opened her eyes. Any man could have *what*? Exacted the same response from her. If *that* was true…

Frenziedly she whirled round and paced the floor. It was because she had been thinking about Gareth… It was *Gareth* who she really wanted…who she loved, and it had been a combination of that love for him and her anger at Seb's obviously intended, if not actually uttered, jibe that she was sexually untouched and frustrated…that she was—oh the shame of it—still a virgin.

How had he guessed…known…? Katie closed her

eyes as a fresh wave of anguish-fuelled despair drenched her.

At her age she was past the stage where her virginity could be considered a praiseworthy indication of her respect for herself and her determination not to rush into sexual experimentation simply for its own sake.

Her discovery while at university that she loved Gareth had prevented her from following the path taken by most of her peers and forming an intimate loving relationship with a fellow student. The result was that now she was almost something of an oddity, an adult who was not really properly a woman at all. Only she knew how left out, how uncomfortable, how ashamed she felt on those occasions when her female family peers and most especially, her twin sister, appeared with that bemused, slightly dazed and wholly femalely smug look in their eyes which said that they had recently enjoyed good sex. But even worse than that were those times when her twin Louise tried to coax her to confide in her.

'Who are you dreaming about?' she had teased Katie the last time they had seen one another. 'Do I *know* him…?'

Katie had shaken her head of course, retreating immediately behind a protective wall of cool hauteur which had left Louise looking both bewildered and hurt. But how *could* she tell her that the man she had been daydreaming over was Louise's own husband?

Determinedly Katie gritted her teeth. What had happened with Seb Cooke had simply been an expression of her very natural longing to be able to offer someone her own sensuality, she was sure of it. A very dangerous expression of course, but the relief of knowing there was a plausible, *acceptable* reason for the way she had let herself go in his arms, the way she had not just responded to him but allowed him to *see* how much he was arousing her, was such that she immediately began to feel more like her normal self.

It would have been unbearable to have had to face him knowing that she had actually wanted Seb. But *he* still thought that, she reminded herself.

Downstairs, Seb was saying his 'goodbyes' to his hostess. Fortunately their stay had only been a brief one as Chrissie was expecting her parents down to visit the following day and she and Guy still had to pick up Anthony from Guy's sister.

He still had no idea what on earth had come over him for those few minutes he had held Katie Crighton in his arms, or rather he was perfectly well aware *what* had, but what he did *not* know was *why* it had. He had known far more forthright women, women who had made it *more* than plain that they would love him to take them to bed, and had been able to turn away from them without even the merest twinge of the savage flood of desire that *Katie* had aroused in him.

Anger and desire. As a scientist he ought to know that there was no more potentially dangerous sexual combination and as a scientist, too, he ought also to know that as a *man* his desire and his arousal were simply physical reactions... Maybe. But as a *man* he *also* knew that what he had felt when he touched Katie had had the same raw, powerful energy that nature herself possessed and as yet man had found no satisfactory way of controlling. Ask any scientist who had tried to find a way of combatting a hurricane, a tidal flood, a volcano or an earthquake... Damn the woman, she was the *last* kind of complication he needed in his life, now or at any time. Even so, just for a moment he allowed himself the luxury of closing his eyes and briefly reliving that moment out of time when she had opened hers and looked at him, her eyes full of shocked liquid pleasure. Had she looked into his and seen there just what he was thinking? Feeling…wanting…? Just how *much* he had yearned to have her then lying naked on a bed beneath him while he licked the damp salt taste of her pleasure from her body and felt her quiver in the aftermath of her orgasm while he did so.

A bad father and a bad husband he might have been, but as Sandra had once openly and frankly told him, as a lover his sensuality had totally overwhelmed her.

A sensual scientist. It was a contradiction in terms, two imperfect halves that when put together rubbed and jarred against one another causing friction and pain.

In the front seat of the car Chrissie commented quietly to Guy, 'Katie still doesn't look very well. I don't think she's been as happy as she used to be since Louise got married… I suppose it must be hard for her, them being twins…'

'Mmm….' Guy agreed. 'She did seem rather subdued, but then she always has been the quieter of the two of them. Well, at least she's got Louise's visit home for Ben's party to look forward to.'

'What did *you* think of her, Seb?' Guy asked and then laughed, 'Or shouldn't we ask? There were certainly some sparks flying between the two or you.'

'I found her rather too idealistic and over-emotional,' Seb responded curtly. 'Not my type at all.'

In their front seats Guy and Chrissie heard Seb's response. It had been unexpectedly curt and did not exactly bode well for Katie and Seb's future as close neighbours.

CHAPTER FIVE

FOR the umpteenth time since she had arrived at work, Katie smoothed down the skirt of her impressively formal black suit. She couldn't remember ever having dressed for work with such anxiety and awareness. This suit was one she had bought in London at Louise's urging and was much more her sort of thing than Katie's own.

The jacket was immaculately tailored, the skirt short and straight. It was an outfit that breathed professionalism and power. In it, with her hair smoothed back she looked, Katie had decided, impressively formidable and there was no way that *anyone*, but most especially Seb Cooke with whom she had an appointment in fifteen minutes' time, was going to get the wrong impression about her attitude towards him. He was a *client* and, of course, that was *all* and she intended to treat him as such.

'Goodness. *You* look smart,' Olivia commented as she walked into the room and did a small double take as she studied Katie's suit. 'Very elegant.'

'It's Armani,' Katie felt impelled to tell her, admitting wryly, 'Louise chose it…'

'Mmm… It's the kind of suit that men visualise a woman wearing with absolutely nothing on underneath,' Olivia murmured teasingly. 'Or so Caspar would have had me believe when I bought one.'

Normally Katie would have taken her comment with a good humoured pinch of salt but the way Seb had behaved towards her, her own reaction to him, their aggression and the passion which had burst into life between them, had put her so much on edge that instead she demanded flatly,

'I hope you aren't serious.'

'Men are *never more* serious than when they're talking about sex,' Olivia responded dryly. 'I promise you that when Caspar saw me wearing what I had innocently imagined was a perfectly respectable and business-like suit to go to court in, he told me that the only "briefs" that would be on everyone's mind in the courtroom would be mine and that in those *male* minds they would most definitely be black and silky. Absurd, I know.' She gave a rueful grimace. 'I had a hard time getting my *own* head round it, but apparently there's a deep in-built male psychological reason for it, something to do with their need to compete with and diminish a woman's worldly power, a throw-back to their childhood when they had to learn to detach themselves from their mothers and learn how to become men... They're quite sad sometimes really, aren't they, poor things,' Olivia continued cheerfully, pausing as their receptionist came in to tell Katie, 'Seb Cooke is here to see you.'

'Mmm... Seb Cooke.' Olivia rolled her eyes naughtily and told Katie robustly,

'Now, in *your* shoes, were *I* single and fancy free, I rather suspect that if I had a Seb Cooke seated across my desk from me, *I'd* be the one doing the mental undressing and the sexy intimate visualisation...'

'Olivia!' Katie protested. 'I'm *not*... He *doesn't*...'

But Olivia was already on her way to her own office, leaving Katie to ask the receptionist to show Seb into her own small cupboard-like room.

She hadn't seen him since the incident at her parents'

home and as he walked in and she indicated to him that he was to sit down, Katie was sharply aware of how relaxed and in control *he* appeared in contrast to her own nervous discomfort.

'This shouldn't take very long,' she told him as crisply and professionally as she could as she, too, sat down. 'The contracts are pretty straightforward and it's only a matter of reading and signing them and then completion can take place virtually immediately.'

'Good. I've got a business conference to attend soon and if possible I want to move in to the apartment beforehand.'

Katie didn't say anything. She, too, ought to have been looking forward to her own occupation of *her* apartment—she *would* have been doing so had it not been for the fact that *he* was going to be her closest neighbour.

Had what happened over the weekend occurred before she had made her decision to buy the apartment, *would* she have changed her mind?

Like her, Seb was wearing a formal business suit, its jacket unfastened over an immaculately laundered crisp, white shirt and a subtly patterned tie. Who *ironed* his shirts? she wondered absently. Surely not Seb himself. Her father had occasionally ironed his own when they were all growing up and he had needed one of his 'court' shirts in a rush. He had even ironed their school shirts once when her mother hadn't been well. Katie could still remember how oddly creased they had remained despite his best efforts, the mystery not being explained until her mother had discovered he had had the iron on the wrong setting.

Seb watched her furrowed forehead as he recognised

both the deliberate distance she was putting between them and her not quite totally hidden anxiety.

What did she think he was? Some kind of potential sexual bully who might pounce on her given the least excuse? There was no point in him saying anything. How *could* he when he couldn't even furnish himself with a rational explanation for what had happened...for what was *still* happening he recognised as she leaned across the desk pushing the contract towards him and he caught the clean, freshly washed scent of her hair and his stomach muscles contracted sharply in reaction to the savage surge of desire that kicked through him.

As she watched Seb virtually openly recoil back from her as she pushed the contract towards him, Katie could feel her body and then her face start to burn with chagrin. What did he think she was going to *do*...flirt with him; come on to him? The urge to tell him that he was wrong, that she loved someone else, was almost overwhelming.

Deliberately keeping her eyes down so that she didn't have to look into his face, she watched him sign the contract. He had very long, strong looking fingers with well-kept clean nails. His hands, while large, possessed a flexibility that for some reason made her heart start to beat far too heavily.

Briefly she closed her eyes and then wished that she had not done so as she had a momentary vision of those hands, *his* hands resting against her own skin, her *naked* skin, stroking and caressing it, cupping the soft flesh of her breasts whilst his fingers...

In her mind's eye she could see the hard darkness of his hand contrasting with the softer paleness of her own flesh. She could *feel* the hot, dizzying ripples of sensation spreading through her body from that point of contact like liquid fire. She could actually see, as though somehow she were standing outside herself as another observer, the way she was lifting her own head and looking at him, focusing on his face…his eyes, his mouth, but what shocked and appalled her most of all was not what she was mentally visualising but the *sensations she was experiencing*—the hot, sharp female pleasure she was feeling…the longing.

Her office was suddenly as claustrophobic as the passageway of her parents' home had been and she could feel the same sense of panic and anxiety beginning to rush through her. She felt hot…faint…weak…and she wanted…

Seb had finished reading the contract, which he had signed and was now passing it back to her. With a tremendous effort of will Katie forced herself to focus on the reality of why he was here in her office.

Seb, meanwhile, was already standing up, patently anxious to leave, but surely not so anxious as she was for him to go.

So why then, as she witnessed his signature, did she have this absurd desire to cry?

Shakily she pushed her own chair back and stood up.

'We'll inform you just as soon as contracts have been exchanged and completion takes place so that you can pick up the keys to your apartment,' she told him quietly.

'I take it you're still going ahead with your own purchase?' Seb asked.

Katie tensed. What was he trying to say? That he had expected her to pull out of her purchase? That he didn't *want* her as his closest neighbour?

Lifting her head she looked him fully in the face for the first time since he had walked into her office.

'Is there any reason why I shouldn't?' she asked him shortly.

To her relief he didn't take up her challenge, instead merely shaking his head and walking away from her towards the door pausing once he got there to tell her, 'I shall be getting in touch with the agents to make arrangements to have the key made available so that measurements can be taken for carpets and curtains.'

'That's a matter for you to sort out with the agents,' Katie told him briefly. 'As your solicitor I have, of course, to tell you that they are under no legal obligation to allow you to have access to the property until completion actually takes place.'

'Indeed,' Seb drawled, equally briefly, opening the door as he informed her dryly, 'However, I wasn't actually *seeking* your *professional* advice, I was simply taking the precaution of warning you as my closest neighbour that should you happen to see anyone coming to or going from my apartment it will merely be the interior designers I'm commissioning to furnish the place for me in case their presence alarmed you.'

Interior designers. Katie digested this information in silence. *She* was planning to call on the combined expertise and advice of her mother and female relatives for help to decorate and furnish her own apartment.

Neither did she have any intention of telling him that the only person whose presence was likely to alarm her was his.

After he had gone she opened the office window and breathed in deep lungfuls of air. But even after she had closed the window she could still smell the subtle scent that was purely *him* and in the end she had to resort to taking her work out into the general office to escape from the effect it was having on her.

*   *   *

'Oh Dad, *please*, I'd *love* to go.'

Seb grimaced a little at being confronted by his daughter's enthusiasm for something he himself had hoped to avoid becoming involved in.

'It is a very special day,' Chrissie told him winningly adding her own form of gentle persuasion to Charlotte's enthusiasm.

'Mmm…and as a member of Aarlston hierarchy here in Haslewich I suspect that you will be expected to put in an appearance,' Guy chimed in.

They were discussing the weekend's forthcoming 'Fun Day' that Aarlston were sponsoring at Fitzburgh Place for the single parents and their families who lived in Ruth Crighton's sheltered accommodation and to which Aarlston employees were also permitted to take their own families.

'Have you met Lord Astlegh yet?' Guy was continuing, and when Seb shook his head Chrissie informed him with a smile,

'You'll like him. He's charming. Very much a gentleman of the old school.'

'Mmm… I can remember scrumping apples from the estate when I was a boy. His gamekeeper certainly wasn't very gentlemanly when he evicted us and threatened us with horrible reprisals if we ever set foot there again,' Seb remembered, looking rueful.

'*You*, scrumping apples? Dad… I *can't* believe it,' Charlotte laughed, shaking her head teasingly.

'Oh, he was quite a young tearaway as a boy,' Guy told Charlotte straight-faced. 'You ask my sister Laura…'

'No such thing,' Seb denied.

'But we are going to the Fun Day, aren't we?' Charlotte coaxed. 'It will be fun.'

As he looked into his daughter's hopeful face, Seb knew that he had no real option.

Although he hadn't shown it he had been thrilled when Charlotte had telephoned earlier in the week to ask if she could spend the weekend with him.

He had finished work a little earlier in order to spend as much time as he could with her and it had been Chrissie's suggestion that they all have dinner together at the restaurant owned and run by Guy's sister Frances and her family.

Charlotte had fast become a favourite with those members of the Cooke family she had met, and if anything she fitted in far better and enjoyed their company much more than he could remember doing as a child, Seb acknowledged.

'So, it's decided then. What time are we going to go?' Charlotte demanded excitedly.

'Well, I'd recommend a reasonably early start,' Guy suggested, but then he paused and frowned and turned to Seb asking him, 'Didn't you say you had someone to see at the apartment in the morning?'

'The interior designer you recommended,' Seb told him. 'I've got this conference coming up and...'

'Oh yes, of course. Well Jamie is very professional. Once you've given her an idea of what you want you'll be able to leave everything safely in her hands.'

'Has Katie Crighton moved into *her* apartment yet?' Charlotte asked Seb interestedly. 'She's nice. I...'

'She'll be moving in next week,' Chrissie told her, adding with a smile, 'She was complaining the other day that Maddy had walked her feet off when she took her on a tour of some fabric warehouses. Maddy is married to Katie's elder brother Max,' Chrissie explained for Charlotte's sake.

'She and Max and their children live at Queensmead which is Ben Crighton's home and I still can't believe how Maddy has managed to turn it from the rather drab and almost unwelcoming house it was into the lovely, warm *home* it is now.'

'I think it's called love,' Guy told her softly.

'Mmm... Well, she's certainly transformed the place. She's marvellously multi-talented and seems to have a gift for finding a good bargain.'

'Katie was telling me that thanks to Maddy, she's found the most wonderful fabric for her curtains at a fraction of the original price.'

The arrival of Frances to chat with them and take their order put a stop to Chrissie's conversation for which Seb was profoundly thankful. He had not seen anything of Katie since he had visited her office to sign his contract and he suspected that she was deliberately avoiding him. He had told himself that he was glad, that the last thing he wanted was the kind of complications in his life that getting involved in any kind of relationship with her would bring him.

He was bound to see her tomorrow though, of course. From what he had heard, the Crighton family would be out in full force at the Fun Day. Ruth Crighton herself was apparently flying over from America with Grant, specially to be there.

'Come on everyone, it's time we were leaving.'

As Katie took a last gulp of her coffee early Saturday morning, she reflected that the annual Fun Day, with the constant stream of arrivals milling about in her parents' comfortable kitchen, was becoming almost as much of an institution as the charity itself.

Up at Queensmead, Maddy would have a full house,

too, and down in the town square the coaches hired to take everyone to Fitzburgh Place would already be filling up with excited children and their families.

One innovative practice that Ruth and Maddy had brought into existence had been the creation of special family rooms within the houses occupied by single mothers and their children so that the men, or more often boys, who had fathered them but who, for one reason or another, had not previously been a part of those children's lives, could be encouraged to visit and establish contact with their children.

Another innovative scheme, recently been put into practice, taught the young parents parenting skills, and Maddy was currently trying to persuade the local secondary school to allow her to establish a scheme that would mean teenage girls and boys became responsible for a computer programmed 'baby doll' which would mimic the responses of a real baby and give them a taste of just what parenthood was *really* all about.

'It's not about frightening them into *not* having sex, but rather of showing them, warning them, just how much an unplanned pregnancy will change their lives,' Maddy had told Katie earnestly when she had been explaining what they hoped to do.

'I'm so pleased that Louise and Gareth were able to make it,' Katie heard her mother enthusing as she expertly loaded empty breakfast dishes into the dishwasher. 'I can't believe how much little Nick has grown.'

Nick was Louise and Gareth's young son and Katie forced herself to smile as her mother started to extol the virtues of her small grandson.

'Goodness, just look at the time,' Jenny Crighton exclaimed. 'Katie, will you run upstairs and warn Louise that we've got to leave in ten minutes.'

By the time Seb and Charlotte reached Fitzburgh Place the Fun Day was in full swing. They had stopped off on the way at the apartment where Seb had arranged to meet the interior designer who, as Guy had promised him, proved to be extremely professional and knowledgeable.

'You want something comfortable and homey,' Charlotte had informed him when Jamie had been asking him about his own preferences for the decor of the apartment. 'Not something high-tech and modern...'

'I want something that's in keeping with the period of the building and the features of the rooms,' Seb told the designer calmly. 'The office you can leave to me... I intend to commission a desk specifically to house my computer and files. Oh, and I shall need a proper bed in the master bedroom, so please make sure it's both large and comfortable.'

'What are you planning to do in there?' Charlotte had teased him. 'Hold orgies?'

'Believe it or not...*sleep*,' Seb had corrected her dryly.

Predictably Charlotte had had her own opinions about how she thought *her* room should be furnished, explaining to the designer just what she wanted and then pausing breathlessly to ask Seb if he approved of her choice.

'I don't mind, just so long as you don't have it Barbie-doll pink...' Seb told her truthfully.

Charlotte had flashed him an indignant look.

'I grew out of *that* years ago, Dad.'

Now, as they left his parked car, Seb surveyed the excited throng of people milling around and reflected that it was just as well that it had turned out to be a warm sunny day.

'Oh look Dad, over there, that must be Katie's twin

sister and her husband,' Charlotte told him tugging on his arm and directing his attention to where a girl who was quite definitely Katie's twin was standing, or rather leaning against the impressively tall man standing with her.

Yes, she was quite definitely Katie's twin, Seb recognised, and yet at the same time he knew that he would have known instantly that she *wasn't* Katie, even without the difference in their hairstyles.

'I wonder where Katie is?' Charlotte mused. 'Perhaps we could go over and ask her sister.'

Seb raised his eyebrows. 'I don't think that's a good idea. Katie will probably be very busy,' he warned her.

Ten minutes later as they walked past the informal crèche, which had been organised for the children, Seb realised that he had been right.

Katie was in the middle of a large circle of children reading them a story oblivious to their presence until Charlotte waved to her.

Although her voice faltered and her face changed colour slightly, she continued with what she was doing causing Seb to suggest to Charlotte that they should move on and leave her in peace.

'No, she's almost finished, but *you* don't have to stay if you want to walk round. I'll catch up with you at the tea stall in half an hour or so,' Charlotte told him.

Shrugging his shoulders Seb left her where she was and walked away to talk with Saul who he had spotted standing several yards away with his family.

'Charlotte,' Katie smiled, as her story finished. Charlotte came hurrying towards her.

'I've just seen your twin sister,' Charlotte told her warmly. 'She was over past the bouncy castle with her husband and the most gorgeous little boy.'

'Their son, Nick,' Katie agreed.

'I think what you're all doing here is wonderful,' Charlotte told her. 'My mother always says how lucky she was that after she and Dad decided their marriage wasn't working out, Dad always made sure that he provided for me financially and then, of course, Mum met George and they fell in love.' She gave Katie a rueful grin.

'Dad tends to beat himself about the chest with guilt a bit because he wasn't there for me when I was growing up, but to tell the truth, George was such a wonderful loving step-father that I didn't even realise for ages that he *wasn't* my birth father, and then once I did... I was curious about Dad of course, but once Ma had explained that she had felt that it would only confuse me and make me feel torn between them both if she encouraged Dad to be there more for me, I felt she'd made the right decision.'

'It was actually *George* who encouraged me to go for it when Dad did contact me. I was apprehensive about how he would react but when Dad explained to me how much he regretted the break-up of his and Mum's marriage and how bad he felt about it and me, how much he'd wanted to make contact with me but hadn't felt that he had the right to do so...

'He and Mum have both said separately to me that they never should have married... They confused lust with love. Have you ever been in love?' she asked Katie curiously.

Too taken aback to feel offended by the intimacy of her curiosity Katie didn't know what to say, but fortunately Charlotte didn't seem to notice her hesitancy, continuing instead,

'I wish that Dad could find someone to love... I think

part of the reason he buried himself in his work when I was a baby was because it was so hard for him to face up to the fact that he and Ma had married for the wrong reasons and that they didn't really love one another,' she told Katie wisely. 'I'd hate to get to Dad's age without ever having loved anyone properly and being loved back by them,' she added abruptly.

She giggled, confiding, 'Dad thinks that every boy I date is going to seduce me, but I'm not ready for that kind of relationship yet. I've got too much to do, but one day soon I *shall* be. Dad has this bit of a thing about the reputation of the Cooke men as wicked seducers. Although he never really talks about it, I think that's why he insisted on marrying Mum instead of just going to bed with her. Of course, I know things were different when they were young but I don't think there's anything wrong in someone wanting to explore their sexuality. It's part of growing up, isn't it?

'When I *do* commit myself to a man, a relationship, I want it to be because I know beyond any kind of doubt that I love him, so I want to make sure that I've got the sex thing sorted out first. I mean for both sexes, losing one's virginity is kind of a very major rite of passage, isn't it, and of course I want it to be with the right person.

'I expect you felt the same when you lost yours,' she added questioningly.

Katie could feel herself floundering, lost in a sticky morass of conflicting emotions and thoughts. Was Charlotte trying to seek her advice or was she simply using her as a sounding board? The age gap between them wasn't huge, but it was enough for Katie to know that in Charlotte's eyes they stood on opposite sides of the chasm that was experience. If only Charlotte knew

the truth. From what she had just said Katie felt that
Charlotte's outlook and attitude towards sex was far
more mature than her own, but then Charlotte wasn't in
love with a man she could never have.

Charlotte's comments about her father had been
equally enlightening, although after the way he had behaved towards her, Katie was finding it extremely hard
to reconcile the man who was so moralistic that he had
married a woman he didn't love with the one who had
behaved so sexually demandingly towards her.

'Hi... I've come to relieve you.'

Katie looked up and smiled as Tullah, Saul's wife,
came up to join them.

'Oh good, that means you can come with me and help
me find Dad,' Charlotte informed Katie as she slipped
her arm through hers.

Find *Seb*! That was the *last* thing Katie wanted to do,
but Charlotte obviously wasn't going to take 'no' for an
answer and so reluctantly Katie found herself walking
beside her as Charlotte led the way to the spot where
she had arranged to meet Seb.

CHAPTER SIX

'LOOK who I've brought with me,' Charlotte told Seb as she gaily wriggled her way through the crowds to his side, tugging Katie after her.

'I'll bet you're dying for something to drink after all that story-telling,' she teased Katie as she slipped her free arm through her father's so that she was standing between them.

'Dad…' she began, but Katie, guessing what was coming and knowing that Seb would have as little appetite for her company as she did for his forestalled Charlotte, telling her quickly, 'No Charlotte, it's alright. My mother has brought a family picnic and she'll be expecting me to join them.'

Oddly as she looked at him, instead of seeming relieved at the prospect of being freed from her company Seb was actually frowning. She was just on the point of disengaging herself from Charlotte when a small boy suddenly dashed towards her carrying a sharp pointed stick which must at one stage have had a balloon attached to it from the strips of brightly coloured plastic dangling from it. It wasn't the burst balloon that caused Katie to dart forward anxiously snatching him up as he started to fall, however, but the knowledge that the sharp end of the stick was potentially dangerous to him.

As she grabbed him he gave a loud wail of protest that quickly turned to a broad beaming smile as Katie deftly distracted his attention by cuddling him and asking him who he was.

'Me Joey,' he told her flashing her an impishly dev-ilish Cooke smile so like Seb's that her heart suddenly lurched against her ribs causing her to miss a breath.

'Joey...there you are...'

Katie turned round as a plump dark-headed woman came hurrying towards them. Immediately Joey stretched out his arms wriggling to be handed over as he cried eagerly,

'Mum...'

'He was going to fall,' Katie told the young woman as she handed him over, not wanting her to think that she had had any ulterior motive in picking him up.

'Yes, I know... I saw you,' the other woman told her. As she cuddled her son her eyes studied Katie; their velvety dark gaze so intense and hypnotic that Katie couldn't drag her own gaze away.

'Here,' the woman added meaningfully as she touched her forehead. 'I sensed he was in danger and then I saw you reaching for him...' Her eyes flashed with pride and hauteur as she saw Katie's expression.

'If you don't believe me ask him,' she told Katie with a small toss of her head looking at Seb. '*He's* one of us and he knows that some of us have the sight...the gift...'

Katie knew it too. The ability for certain female mem-bers of the Cooke clan to foretell future events was a well documented local fact, but this was the first time *she* personally had been the focus of witnessing it in action.

'I wasn't doubting you,' Katie reassured her, gently reaching out her hand to smooth the little boy's tangled curls. His hair was dark like his mother's—like Seb's—and wonderfully soft to touch. Seb's child... Seb's son would have just such hair. For a moment she thought she must be falling under some extraordinary spell the gypsy woman had cast, for unbelievably she suddenly had a mental image of Seb's child, as potent and lifelike as though he actually already existed. But almost immediately her common sense reasserted itself and she told herself that she was simply being over-imaginative.

But then, just as they were about to walk away, the gypsy woman reached for Katie's arm and told her softly, nodding in Charlotte's direction,

'She is not a child you have made together but there *will* be one and very soon.'

Releasing Katie she turned to Seb who had listened to the entire exchange in silence.

'*You* do not believe me, but it is true,' she told him fiercely. 'Give me your hand,' she instructed Katie, reaching for it and taking hold of it before she could draw back from her.

It was ridiculous of her to feel that she was in the presence of a mystical power as awesome and ancient as life itself Katie acknowledged, and yet that *was* how she felt as the girl pored over her hand and then pronounced firmly, 'It is written quite clearly here. You are one another's fates, although neither of you has recognised it yet, but before you can do so, you,' she told Seb, turning to him and addressing him almost sharply, 'must close the door on what you are using to deny yourself your future. There is no need for it, no place for it. And you,' she told Katie a little more gently, 'must close the door on that which you know can never rightfully belong to you...'

For a moment none of them spoke. A stillness—a silence—seemed to envelop them like an invisible cloak and then excitedly Charlotte was holding out her hand to the girl pleading, 'What about me? What can you see in *my* hand?'

The woman's expression lightened as she released Katie's hand and took hold of Charlotte's.

'I see that you still have a long journey to complete along the path of knowledge before you begin your life's work. And I see, too...' Very gently she closed Charlotte's fingers over her palm and then told her slowly, 'I see that you will be among those who will give to the world a very great deal of good.'

And then abruptly she released Charlotte's hand and was gone, disappearing into the swirling crowd leaving the three of them to stand in silence while they digested her predictions.

'Well...' Charlotte gasped. 'Wasn't that *extraordinary*... Did you notice her eyes? I felt almost as though she was hypnotising me.'

'She probably was, or at least attempting to do so,' her father told her curtly, adding grimly, 'It's all rubbish, of course.'

'I really must go,' Katie told them both. There was absolutely no way she could bring herself to look at Seb, not after what the girl had said. Seb was right, it *had* all been rubbish, a piece of ineffective guesswork on the other woman's part based on the fact that they were together. She had probably assumed that they were already a couple and that Katie, who quite obviously couldn't be Charlotte's mother, *must* want to have Seb's child herself. It was silly for her to feel so hyper-sensitively aware of that mental image she had had of that small dark-haired boy so very, very like Seb. That had simply been a coincidence that was all.

'She obviously thought that the two of you were a couple,' Charlotte commented with a wide smile.

'No.'

'No way...'

Charlotte looked from her father to Katie and then back again as they both uttered their denials at the same time.

'Oh, but you heard what she said,' she teased. 'It's inevitable...*fate*...'

'I'd say the explanation is much closer to hand and owes far more to a vivid imagination than any supernatural influence,' Seb announced dryly.

'Katie—there you are. Ma has sent us to look for you so that we can eat lunch.'

With the sudden appearance of Louise, with Gareth at her side and their son in his arms, it was tempting to tell Seb that he was wrong and that a certain mischievous and even malign unseen force appeared to enjoy wreaking havoc with her composure, but of course Katie knew she would do—could do—no such thing, not without revealing just *why* the arrival of her twin sister with her husband and baby should be so uncomfortable for her.

It was normal custom in the Crighton family and most especially her own generation of it for both its female and male members to embrace, hug and kiss one another in greeting, but after the first time she had frozen back in anguish when Gareth had attempted to hug her when he and Louise had become a couple. Gareth had always kept his distance from her and Katie had been profoundly grateful to him for doing so. But contradictorily on this occasion, all too aware of Seb's keen eyes and Charlotte's curious ones on them, she almost wished that he would step forward and give her a brotherly hug.

Of course introductions had to be made and while Charlotte cooed enthusiastically over Nick, Gareth and Seb exchanged male pleasantries, each patently calmly assessing the other.

'You'll never *guess* what's just happened,' Charlotte

started to tell Louise excitedly, while Katie's heart sank. Only let her twin get wind of what the girl had predicted... But to her relief instead of immediately teasing them both over the girl's prediction, Louise was uncharacteristically tactful and silent on the subject, simply reiterating their parents were waiting to begin lunch.

'Mmm...lunch, that sounds like a good idea, Dad,' Charlotte told her father enthusiastically. 'I'm starving...'

As she saw the rather rueful look Seb was giving the fast food outlets close by, Louise suggested promptly,

'Look, why don't you join us. Knowing Ma there'll be more than enough...'

'Oh, no...'

'Thank you, but no...'

As both Seb and Katie spoke together, Louise raised her eyebrows a little, her attention focusing rather too keenly for Katie's liking on what she knew to be her give-away flushed face.

But before she or Seb could reiterate their rejections of Louise's suggestion, Guy and Chrissie were coming towards them.

'I was just inviting Sebastian and Charlotte to join us for lunch,' Louise explained immediately to her mother's ex-business partner.

'You were...that's good because I've just seen Jenny myself and accepted her invitation that the five of us should join you...'

Her heart sinking Katie automatically turned to go to her sister's side but as she did so, Guy asked her apologetically, 'Katie, would you mind taking your father's keys and going to the car to get the cutlery your mother asked me to collect. Anthony needs changing before lunch and our car is parked on the other side of the field, so...'

Only too glad to have an opportunity to get away from Sebastian Cooke, Katie immediately nodded her head and took her father's car keys from Guy.

'We're in our usual picnic spot,' Louise told her sister cheerfully as she fell into step beside Chrissie to exchange mother and baby stories.

Katie had gone less than a few dozen yards when she suddenly heard Seb calling her name.

Turning round she watched warily as he hurried to catch up with her.

'I just wanted to have a few words with you before we join the rest of your family for lunch,' he told her curtly. 'All that rubbish that fake "fortune teller" was spouting had absolutely nothing to do with me,' he informed her unnecessarily.

Immediately Katie could feel her temper starting to burn.

'Well, I certainly didn't have anything to do with her predictions,' she snapped back immediately. 'The very idea is ridiculous. For a start we'd have to...'

She stopped, her face going scarlet at the unexpectedly explicit mental images of just what they would have to do to make the woman's predictions come true filled her mind.

'We'd have to what?' Seb picked up softly for her. 'Go to bed together. Is that what you were going to say?'

Primly Katie looked away from him before answering in a very stifled voice, 'Actually no. What I was going to say is that we would have to...to have a very different relationship from the one we do have...'

'Like I said, we'd have to go to bed together,' Seb

told her succinctly. 'And there's no way that's going to happen.'

Katie couldn't help it, she gave a small gasp of chagrined pride as he delivered his immediate and unequivocal rejection of her.

'You're right,' she agreed quickly and decisively. 'It isn't. The kind of man I would want...the kind of man I find attractive,' she hastily amended, 'Is...would be...'

'Would be what?' Seb challenged her sharply.

Katie was too caught up in her feelings to be either cautious or tactful.

'He wouldn't be anything like you,' she told him pointedly. 'He'd be kind...gentle...caring...' Her voice softened betrayingly, her eyes suddenly remote and dreamy as she continued a little huskily, 'He'd be wise and...and understanding and he'd...he'd never...' She stopped and then told him fiercely, 'he would never, ever, be anything, anyone...like you...'

'No, he wouldn't,' Seb agreed grittily. 'Not me, nor any other red-blooded male. He sounds more like some mythical sexless cardboard cut-out of a man than the real thing,' he told her scathingly. 'A fictional hero who bears as much resemblance to a real man as...'

'You're just saying that because you're not like that,' Katie interrupted him defiantly. 'There are men like that...men who...'

'Men who what?' Seb immediately challenged her, falling into step beside her as Katie, fearing that she was losing ground in their argument turned on her heel and started to hurry towards the field in which her parents' car was parked.

'Let go of me,' she protested as Seb reached for her arm when she continued to ignore him.

'Not until you've answered my question,' he told her

grimly. 'Men who what? Tell me exactly what it is about this mythical mate you deem so desirable—because it certainly can't be his sexuality.'

'Seb!' Katie flashed back at him immediately. 'There's more to a relationship…to love…than that…'

'Indeed there is, but I think you'll find most men— and women—want the pleasure of enjoying and arousing their chosen partner's sexual desires. You must have experienced that for yourself,' he continued curtly when Katie made no response other than tensing in his grasp as they both came to a halt opposite one another. His expression changed subtly as he looked down into her wary eyes.

'You have experienced it, haven't you, Katie?' he asked her softly.

'What I have or have not experienced is no concern of yours.' Katie defended herself valiantly.

'Perhaps not,' Seb agreed, but instead of releasing her and turning away as she had expected, he suddenly moved closer to her causing her stomach to turn in anxious protest. 'Or perhaps our fortune-teller does know something that you and I do not… Shall we find out…?'

'No…' Katie started to protest, but it was too late. Cloaked as they were by the shadows cast by the trees at the edge of the field it was dangerously easy for Seb to draw her fully into his arms, imprisoning her there as he bent his head and his mouth came down expertly and inescapably over hers.

It was a kiss more of anger and retribution than anything else, Katie was not so naive that she didn't recognise that fact.

He had resented the fortune-teller's prediction and he was angry with her because he didn't like her and this was his way of punishing her.

'No…' she managed to protest sharply against his mouth as she struggled to break free of him, her teeth accidentally grazing his bottom lip as she did so.

'What the…'

As she heard him curse Katie froze. She could taste the slight saltiness of his blood on her own tongue and was horrified by what she had done, even if he had provoked it.

'…and what you want is a gentle passive lover,' she heard him demanding savagely. 'You're a liar, Katie. You want a man whose passion matches your own, a man who…'

'What I don't want is you,' Katie told him frantically.

'And I don't want you,' Seb assured her sharply, his expression changing and holding her in paralysing thrall he added rawly, 'but I want this…'

Katie whimpered in protest as his mouth possessed hers, possessed it, seduced it…ravished it…the pressure of his mouth on hers making her own lips feel so sensitive that her whole body shook with the tiny quivers of sensation she was feeling.

Through the dapple of the leaves on the trees she could feel the warmth of the sun on her face but its heat was nothing to the heat Seb was generating inside her.

She tried to break free of him. She knew she had to. Why were her arms entwined around him, why was her body pressed so close to him, why was her mouth parting beneath the pressure of his…why…?

'See, I told you you were passionate,' she could hear Seb telling her huskily. 'The only reason you'd ever want a meek and mild apology for a mate is so that you could destroy and devour him like a praying mantis…'

'Oh…'

As the cruelty of his words jerked her back to reality, Katie pulled away from him.

'You were the one who... I did nothing,' she amended quickly, unable to look at him.

'Nothing...'

As she attempted to move away from him Seb reached out, cupping her jaw in his hand and turning her face up so that he could look down at her.

'Then, what's this,' he demanded, lifting her hand to his mouth and pressing her fingers against the bruised rawness of his bottom lip.

Giving a small, choked protest Katie pulled away. Her eyes were beginning to fill with tears. She was dizzy and lightheaded and somewhere deep inside her there was a small insidious ache that frightened and shocked her.

But before she could say or do anything she heard Guy's familiar voice calling out semi-scoldingly,

'There you are you two, Jenny thought you must have got lost...'

Later Katie assumed that she must have said and done everything that was expected and required of her during lunch. Certainly no one seemed to find her behaviour odd or out of character, but she herself was intensely, uncomfortably aware of Sebastian Cooke's presence all through the light-hearted alfresco family meal. While the others were chatting and exchanging pleasantries and banter, she was finding it hard to force down so much as a mouthful of her mother's delicious cold spread.

In fact, she noticed a little bitterly at one point, Seb seemed more at ease and relaxed than she did and as for Charlotte...it was plain that she was enjoying herself hugely. Katie could hear her telling Jenny enthusiastically how much she was enjoying life at her sixth form college.

'Being a boarder there makes it even better,' she gushed. 'The other girls are great and I've made so many new friends.'

'It must have been quite a difficult decision for you to make,' Jenny remarked to Seb.

'It was,' he agreed. 'Sandra, George and I all sat down with Charlotte to discuss it. I know she believes at sixteen that she's an adult, but while we accept that she is mature enough to make most of her own decisions about her education, it is an unfortunate fact that this modern world we live in is not always a very safe place for a young woman.

'However, the school has an excellent policy which allows the girls some freedom while at the same time ensuring their safety.'

'Yes, we're allowed evening exeats and we can even go clubbing, just so long as there's a group of eight or more of us and we all come back together in the school minibus.

'Mum and George and Dad did take a bit of persuading to allow me to go, but it's the best "A" level college in the country for my subjects and since I'm hoping to get a place at Manchester University it made sense to move here.'

With her own cousin and younger brother at a very similar stage in their education Katie was not surprised that her mother should be so interested in Charlotte's 'A' level studies, but she wished her mother would not be quite so warm and welcoming towards Sebastian Cooke.

She was uncomfortably aware that by some fluke of circumstance, the group of adults around the picnic had separated themselves out so that she was actually now sitting closer to Seb than she was to anyone else. Unfortunately, the nearest other person to her was Gareth and she had determined to remove any remaining longings for him from her life by keeping as much distance—in every sense of the word—between herself and her brother-in-law as she could.

Still, at least she could comfort herself that Louise had not told the rest of the family about the fortune-teller's prediction and Louise, Katie fervently hoped, would never refer to it again.

However later in the day Katie discovered that her relief had been premature.

At Louise's insistence she had driven her over to see her new apartment while Gareth had been left behind to bathe and feed Nick.

'It's *fabulous*,' Louise pronounced once the short tour was over and they were standing in the apartment's living room. 'When do you expect to move in?'

'Well, hopefully by the end of the week. The carpets should be down by then, although I'm not sure whether or not all the curtains will be finished, but Mum has offered to lend me some in the interim if they aren't.'

'Mmm... It's a *very* sophisticated bachelor-girl place,' Louise approved. 'Although...' with a twinkle in her eye she told Katie, 'Although, if what your *gypsy* friend predicted is true...'

'Seb and I...' Katie interrupted her quickly. 'We...'

But before she could finish her denial Louise was reaching out to touch her, asking her seriously and quietly, 'Can we talk? Properly, I mean...'

Katie's heart sank. This was the moment she had been

dreading ever since Gareth and Louise had announced their love for one another.

'Of course…' she responded with what she knew was a forced note of jollity in her voice. 'What do you want to talk about? We…'

'Katie, come on…this is *us*…you and me… Look, I know…'

Katie froze. Louise knew *what*? That she, Katie, loved *her* husband…?

But, instead of continuing Louise shook her head and said huskily, 'We used to be so *close*, you and I. We told one another *everything*…but since Gareth and I married… You're my *twin*… I still *need* you… I always will and I *hate* feeling that there's this distance, this *barrier* between us. If I've said or done something to hurt you…'

'No. No, of course you haven't,' Katie denied quickly, terrified in case Louise continued to question her and somehow discovered the truth. It wasn't *her* fault that she, Katie, loved Gareth. It wasn't *anyone's* fault, except her own and the last thing she wanted to do was to widen the rift which Louise had so correctly pinpointed by admitting how she really felt. All that admitting her feelings could do would be to embarrass Louise and Gareth and to humiliate herself.

'It's just…' She stopped, frantically hunting for a satisfactory explanation to silence her sister's questions. 'Well, obviously things are different now that you and Gareth are married and that you have Nick.'

'Well, yes, of course,' Louise agreed, her mouth curling into a wide smile as she laughed. 'Still, by the sound of it, it won't be long before you and Seb have a child of your own… He's gorgeously sexy, Katie. *Seriously* sexy,' she underlined, rolling her eyes appreciatively. 'And if I weren't so very much in love with Gareth...'

'Louise, Seb and I...' Katie began frantically, appalled by the direction the conversation was taking and the assumptions Louise had so mistakenly leapt to.

'It's a pity the two of you didn't discover you were in love before you bought this place though. Still it's obvious that you'll make a good profit on it when you sell it. Have you made any plans yet, or...'

'Louise, we barely *know* one another,' Katie protested. 'I don't even...' Like him, never mind love him, she had been about to say but typically Louise wasn't giving her time to finish her conversation before continuing enthusiastically, 'I could see how much Charlotte has taken to you as well. That's wonderful. Mind you, you're so gentle and loving that you'd be able to cope with even the most difficult of step-children and anyone can see that Charlotte is not that. And, of course, it couldn't be better, you and Seb living so close to one another.'

'Louise...' Katie began desperately and then stopped as Louise glanced out of the window and exclaimed,

'Oh, here's Gareth. He must have wondered why we've been gone for so long. Oh Katie, I'm just *so* happy for you,' Louise told her excitedly and she turned to embrace her twin in a loving hug. 'I can tell you now that there was a time when I wondered...well, you were always so determined to defend Gareth in the early days when I was so antagonistic towards him, and I suppose because we *are* twins and because *I* love him so much, I worried that you might...'

With every word Louise spoke Katie could feel her anxiety and anguish growing. It lay like a block of ice against her heart; weighed like the heaviest of lead weights on her conscience. It was all her worst fears come to life. Louise had intuitively sensed her own feelings despite *everything* she had done to try to prevent her from doing so. Louise was her twin, her other half, and there existed between them a bond which called forth from Katie, not just her fiercest loyalty, but also a need to put Louise's needs above her own, to protect her from the hurt and pain that knowing that she, Katie, loved Gareth would cause her. She struggled with her conscience not wanting to deceive her twin but as she already knew, it was almost impossible to stop Louise once she took hold of an idea and started to run with it. And, after all, the truth would very quickly become apparent—it was so obvious that she and Seb loathed one another.

'And you won't forget about your grandfather's party, will you?' Jenny Crighton reminded Louise as she kissed her goodbye.

They had brought the car across from Belgium and were driving on to see Gareth's family in Scotland before returning to Brussels. As she hugged her mother, Louise promised her, 'We'll be there. How could we possibly miss it when it will be Katie's first formal opportunity to show Seb off to the family?'

'Seb?' Jenny questioned in surprise, 'But...'

'I could see that there was something between them straightaway,' Louise continued happily, 'and I'm just so glad for Katie, Mum. She's been so unlike her normal self just lately. That's worried me. It's funny the way things work out, isn't it?' she continued conversationally. 'If she hadn't had to give up her old job because of that awful boss who was making life so miserable for

her, she would never have come home and then she
wouldn't have met Seb.

'You should have seen her face when Charlotte told
us what the girl at the fair had predicted for her and
Seb,' Louise had chuckled. 'A baby boy no less,' she
enlightened her bemused parent. 'Charlotte was thrilled
to bits. No potential problems there, that's *very* clear,
but then Charlotte's almost a young woman herself and
since, from what Guy told me, Seb and his ex-wife's
divorce was mutually agreed and they get on tolerably
well together, at least Katie won't be walking into an
unpleasant situation.

'She's so sensitive, *too* sensitive for her own good I
sometimes think. She always puts other people's feelings
and other people's needs above her own.'

'Yes, she does,' Jenny agreed soberly.

It was news to her that Katie was romantically involved with Seb Cooke, but Louise was quite correct
when she stated that Katie had been unlike her normal
self over the last year or so. Always quiet she had become to a mother's anxious eye worryingly withdrawn,
and it had been at least in part because of her concern
that Jenny had suggested to Jon that they persuade Katie
to come home and join the family business when she
admitted that she was thinking of changing her job.

Not that Jenny had any objections to Seb Cooke as a
prospective son-in-law, far from it. She had taken to him
virtually immediately and she thought that Charlotte was
a honey. No. What *did* surprise her was that her normally
hesitant and even reticent daughter should have committed herself so immediately.

'Oh, yes, Guy, I'm sure that Katie would be thrilled with
it,' Jenny enthused as she studied the pretty little desk

which Guy had invited her to come and see. The antiques shop they had originally begun as a joint venture was now managed by one of Guy's many relatives, Didi Fowler, while Guy concentrated on the other aspects of his small financial empire.

'I remember how much she loved the one I found for my sister Laura,' Guy agreed, 'and when Didi said that this one had come in I thought of Katie and her new apartment straight away. When does she actually move in, by the way? I know that Seb has terminated the lease on his rented property and that he intends to start living in his apartment on his return from this conference he's gone to.'

'Katie said that she'd like to move in as soon as she can and, of course, now that she and Seb are seeing one another I imagine she'll want to move in when he does.'

'Katie and Seb?' Guy whistled soundlessly. 'I hadn't *realised*...' he began and then shook his head.

'Neither had I,' Jenny admitted. 'But Katie confided in Louise and Louise mentioned it to me without realising that Katie hadn't said anything yet herself.'

'A Cooke and a Crighton...that will cause something of a stir. Ben isn't going to like it. How is he by the way...?'

'Not too good, I'm afraid,' Jenny told him worriedly. 'Maddy says he's becoming increasingly distressed about David's absence—we don't use the word "disappearance" around Ben, we never have done, it upsets him so much. You know how much he's always thought of David. He was always the favoured son.'

'Mmm... If you ask me, that was probably the root of David's problem. It wasn't just that Ben had such high expectations of him, it was that he gave David the belief that he had the right to expect the world to place him on the same pedestal his father had done. Well, personally, I can't see how he could ever come back.'

'It wouldn't be easy,' Jenny admitted, 'for any of us. But I can't help wishing for Ben's sake if nothing else that he would at least get in touch with us... In truth, Guy, I'm afraid that if David leaves it too much longer it could well be too late,' she told him sombrely. 'The doctors say there's no valid reason why Ben shouldn't have made a much better recovery from his last operation than he has. In theory he's got every reason to have done so. Just on the basis of the dedicated nursing Maddy's given him, and we had all hoped that having Max based in Chester and living permanently at Queensmead would help—you know that after David, Max has always been his favourite.'

'But Max isn't the person he originally was any longer, is he? Max is much more Jon's son now than he's David's nephew.'

'Yes. As Max himself would be the first to say, what he went through in Jamaica was very much a "Saul on the road to Damascus" conversion for him.' The seriousness left Jenny's eyes and she laughed, explaining to Guy, 'Little Leo must have heard his father using that particular phrase himself because he asked Max what his Uncle Saul was doing on the road to Damascus.'

When they had both finished laughing, Guy went over and patted the desk they had been admiring and told Jenny in amusement, 'Perhaps I should keep this and present it to Katie as a wedding present.

'Seb's a good man,' he told her reassuringly. 'Very highly principled which will suit Katie.'

Having confirmed to Jenny that he would keep the desk for her daughter, Guy went home to tell his wife that they might shortly expect to be celebrating another wedding in the family.

'Seb and Katie. Oh, that's wonderful,' Chrissie enthused. 'Charlotte will be thrilled. She's really taken to Katie,' she added, reiterating Louise's comment to her mother earlier.

Meanwhile, totally unaware of the future being mapped out for them, the two supposed lovers were both independently going about their daily business.

Katie had a busy day filled with appointments all morning and an appearance at court in the afternoon, while Seb was on his way to attend a large conference on the moral implications resulting from the giant strides forward the scientific world was currently making in the field of genetics.

Seb's last telephone call before he had left had been to the interior designer giving her the go-ahead on the designs she had submitted to him. He would be gone less than a week but she had assured him that, given her contacts, enough of the work would be completed to enable him to move into the apartment on his return.

The conference was being held in Florida. Not an ideal venue so far as Seb was concerned, not with the long flight involved. Closing his eyes he settled back in his seat preparing to go to sleep using a relaxation technique he had perfected over the years, but for once neither his mind nor his body were prepared to respond to the commands he was giving them. Instead, behind his closed eyelids, an image formed of the last person he wanted to think about.

Infuriatingly, instead of achieving his normal Zen-like state of pre-sleep calm, Katie Crighton's features kept forming themselves in a series of intimate pictures, the most disconcerting of which set Katie's eyes and hair and mouth in the tousled-haired solemn-expressioned face of a small boy child.

'Oh, no. Oh, no way, no way at all.'

Seb wasn't aware that he had muttered his denial out aloud until he saw the curious look the man in the adjacent seat was giving him.

Scientifically he knew it was totally impossible for anyone to 'see' into the future—true, they *could* make accurate assumptions based on the hard evidence of given facts—and it was perhaps predictable that the gypsy woman should have assumed that he and Katie were a couple and therefore, that she should at some stage bear his child, but there had been something, not so much about her predictions, but about the woman herself that had touched an almost primeval chord inside him.

He shifted uncomfortably in his seat. All right, why not acknowledge it—*admit* it to himself, he *did* want Katie. Sexually she pressed buttons he had forgotten he had long ago, if in fact he had ever known.

Sex for him, while a pleasurable experience, had never driven him, never obsessed him, never *possessed* him as it did some men. Because his awareness of how people viewed Cooke men and their supposedly uncontrollable sexuality had subconsciously made him determined that he would not just rise above the low expectations people had of his family academically, but also determined to rise above the taint of their notorious sexual profligacy.

It was because of that that he had insisted on corralling his youthfully sexual desire for Sandra within the acceptable, *respectable* confines of marriage. Time and experience might have shown him the foolishness of that, but he had never again allowed his sexual desire to get out of control or indeed to have any real input into his life.

Since he had passed thirty he had come to consider himself as a man who had the maturity and the ability to treat the sexual side of his nature as less important to him and with less value to his life than the cerebral satisfaction it gave him to distance himself from any power it might have threatened to have over him.

Now, irritatingly, ridiculously, here he was at thirty-eight discovering that, far from being a thoroughly tamed and unimportant facet of his nature, it had become an out of control hydra-headed monster that sprouted ten new heads for every one he destroyed. Right now, for instance, he had gone from visualising Katie to remembering how it had felt to kiss her; how soft and warm her skin had felt, her breast...how betrayingly her nipple had pulsed and her breathing quickened...how betrayingly, too, she had flushed and looked away, unable to meet his eyes when the gypsy had spouted all that rubbish about them being a couple. Oh yes, she was as physically and intimately aware of *him* as *he* was of her, although he doubted that she had gone as far as entertaining, *envisaging*, the kind of sexual fantasies about him that were plaguing him about her.

Charlotte had been conceived by accident, the result of a missed birth control pill, her conception something neither he nor Sandra had recognised until several weeks later. But if he was to father a child *now*, he would want to *know* it, *sense* it, *feel* it, share with Katie the knowledge that the heat of their passion had ignited the spark that was life.

What the *hell* was he doing...thinking? Catching the passing stewardess's eye Seb ordered the drink he had refused earlier. He must be suffering from some kind of altitude sickness. Either that or that damned gypsy had put some kind of spell on him. Disbelievingly he closed his eyes. Now he knew he was *really* losing it. Spells, predictions...these were things that belonged to the superstitious, the Middle Ages, to a time when people had still believed that the world was flat. He was a scientist, for heaven's sake.

CHAPTER SEVEN

'IT's beginning to look like home already.'

Whirling round Katie hugged her mother gratefully.

Jenny had just spent the best part of the afternoon hanging the curtains she and Maddy had made for Katie's sitting room.

'This damask really looks wonderful,' Jenny murmured, adding feelingly, 'Mind you, it was murder to sew... I've been trying to persuade your father that we ought to give the drawing room a face-lift and this fabric would be perfect.'

'Mmm...it even looks as though it could be antique,' Katie enthused. 'And I love this soft gold colour.'

'Mmm... Maddy has a very good eye. It goes perfectly with your carpet.'

The carpet which had been fitted throughout the apartment was like the curtain fabric, a bargain tracked down by Maddy. Originally ordered by another customer and dyed to her specification, the order had been cancelled when the customer had decided at the last minute that she wanted a different colour.

Her expensive mistake had been Katie's lucky bargain. The soft, pale gold plain wool might not have been to everyone's taste, nor particularly practical, but as both Maddy and Jenny had reassured her she was hardly likely to have much dirt trodden into it living in a top floor apartment.

It had been at Maddy's suggestion that Katie had been persuaded to spend what she had considered to be a very large sum of money on a wallpaper border to go beneath the room's elegant coving. The border, formal swags of gold on a cream background was, Katie had to admit, perfect with the carpet and curtains and she had liked Maddy's suggestion, too, that she might stencil rope tassels on either side of the chimney.

However, rather than employ a decorator she had decided to paste them up herself. An old sofa, again unearthed by Maddy from the attics at Queensmead, was currently being re-upholstered and the bits of furniture which her parents had donated were already in place, along with the double bed she had bought.

'I've hung the old curtains from the guest bedroom at home in your bedroom for now. They'll do until you find a fabric you like. Come and have a look at them.'

As Katie followed her mother into her bedroom Jenny looked at the bed and remarked dryly,

'Wouldn't a king-sized one have been better? I know your father always complained that our old double was too small and Seb's a good inch or so taller than him.'

Speechlessly Katie stared at her mother, the colour draining from her face.

'Louise told me,' Jenny said gently.

'Louise *told* you,' Katie croaked in shock. 'Louise told you about...'

'...about you and Seb. Yes,' her mother confirmed.

Walking over to Katie she put her arms around her and hugged her tenderly.

'I'm so pleased for you, darling. I didn't want to say anything but...well, I know these last couple of years haven't been very happy ones for you. Of course, your grandfather isn't exactly thrilled, not with Seb being a Cooke, but then I'm sure that Seb will be more than a

match for Ben. You've both been summoned to present
yourselves to him at his party, needless to say.'

Katie had to sit down. Why? *Why* hadn't she cau-
tioned Louise not to say anything? *Why* hadn't she realised what would happen if she didn't? This was dreadful.
Awful. Worse than the very worst possible nightmare
she could ever have conjured up. Worse than Louise
discovering that you love Gareth? an inner voice demanded grittily. No, not worse than that. With this, the
only person who would be hurt would be her. What on
earth was she *going* to do? Thank *goodness* Seb was
safely out of the way, out of the country. Somehow she
was going to have to find the courage to tell her mother
that Louise had got it wrong—and before Seb came
back.

Taking a deep breath she closed her eyes and then
said shakily,

'Mum…'

But it was too late, her mother was already speaking.
'When I told Guy he wasn't sure whether or not he ought
to keep the desk for a wedding present, but…'

'Guy knows…' Katie interrupted her hollowly.

Her mother nodded her head.

'Mmm… Apparently Chrissie wasn't all that surprised…'

Silently Katie looked at her mother, totally unable to
find the words to express the enormity of the situation
she was in.

Guy knew!

Chrissie knew!

Everyone, it seemed, knew that she had told her twin
that she and Seb were in love. Lovers, in fact, to judge
from her mother's unexpectedly frank comment about
her double bed earlier…

Everyone… Everyone *except* Seb. A feeling of sick panic filled her. What was she going to do? Even if she told her mother the truth now, it was far too late to stop what was going on getting to Seb's ears. Even if she admitted, retracted, everything, he was bound to hear something. Heaven alone knew how many people were already involved.

She could plead with her own family for silence and, yes, even with Guy and Chrissie, but they were in almost daily contact with Guy's family. Guy's family, like Seb's were Cookes.

Katie could almost see news of their supposed relationship spreading and gathering momentum as it did so, so that she could easily envisage some distant Cooke connection working at the airport who might greet Seb with the news of his impending marriage to her on his arrival back in the country.

She was beginning, Katie decided, to feel extremely ill and she could well understand what had prompted Victorian women to go into a decline. If only there had been some convenient convent, preferably one belonging to a silent order, for her to disappear into.

'Heavens, is that the time? I *must* go,' her mother was saying. 'Your father will be wondering where on earth I am.'

Weakly Katie got up and accompanied her mother to the door. Once she had gone, Katie walked into her immaculate, hand-painted, newly finished kitchen. She had never been much of a drinker but right now she was badly in need of something restorative and courage-boosting. The only alcohol she had though was the moving-in gift of half a dozen bottles of good wine from her father.

This was all the fault of that woman. If *she* hadn't

made that prediction... Reluctantly Katie forced herself to acknowledge that she was being unfair. The blame lay fairly and squarely on her own shoulders, firstly for having involved Seb and secondly for not correcting Louise. Now her own weaknesses were being held over her head like a veritable sword of Damocles, waiting, not so much to fall but to be brought down on her un-protected neck by the full weight of Seb's fury.

In the meantime she might as well occupy herself un-packing and putting away her possessions.

Several hours later she was just closing the last of the drawers in her bedroom, the scent of the lavender bags she had placed among her things making her smile rue-fully.

The lavender was from her mother's garden and just to smell it evoked memories of hers and Louise's child-hood.

If there could be a silver lining to the leaden weight of the cloud threatening her then it had to be the closing of the rift which had sprung up between her and Louise.

Seeing Gareth had hurt as it always did, but oddly this time, the hurt had been less intense, more a soft ache rather than a sharp agony, her daydreams of him as her lover somehow dulled and put out of focus by the far stronger acid-sharp bite of the sensual passion she had felt for Seb.

But that had just been sex and she loved Gareth... Loved...past tense... Katie started to frown.

The conference had been very demanding, they always were, but normally Seb found such concentration chal-lenging and adrenalin-releasing, a recharge. This time, concentrating on the speeches had been hard work and yet, conversely, he somehow hadn't been able to give them his full attention, his thoughts constantly performing clever tricks to take him where he didn't want to go.

Katie Crighton!

By now she would no doubt have moved into her apartment where she would be his closet neighbour, where they would be living as intimately as though...

Abruptly Seb put a clamp on his thoughts. His mood, already affected detrimentally by what he considered to be his own weakness, hadn't been improved by the long flight nor the delay waiting for his luggage at Manchester.

Guy, who had offered to pick him up from the airport, saw him coming out of the Arrivals hall. He went to meet him exclaiming, 'Cheer up. Mind you, I suppose you'd much rather have had Katie picking you up than me.'

Stopping abruptly—so abruptly that the man behind him almost walked into him—Seb demanded sharply,

'Katie! What?'

'Mmm... The pair of you have created *quite* a stir *I* can tell you. A Cooke marrying a Crighton... Chrissie's got Crighton blood too, of course, but she isn't a "Crighton Crighton". I'd have loved to have seen old Ben's face when they gave him the news. Jenny says he's demanding that the pair of you put in an appearance at his party.'

Quickly Seb assimilated what Guy was saying and then demanded ominously,

'Are you telling me that the whole town...?'

'..knows that you and Katie are an item? Yes, I'm afraid so,' Guy agreed ruefully. 'That's what comes of being a member of such a large extended family. I wouldn't even think of trying to deny it if I were you,' Guy counselled him with a grin. 'The females of the family are already planning a mass exodus to Chester to hunt for wedding outfits.

'Pity the pair of you had agreed to buy your apartments before you declared your feelings for one another. It could be hard work for Katie with a baby carriage up and down those stairs, especially if our gypsy relative has got it wrong and her "one" turns out to be "two",' Guy told him with a wicked grin, adding mock-sagely, 'After all *someone* has to be the first to provide the Crightons with the next generation's pair of twins.'

'Twins.' Seb frowned.

'Yes, twins, you know, two babies who are identical to one another,' Guy told him helpfully, tongue in cheek. 'Twins like your Katie and Louise. According to Jenny it was Louise who wheedled it out of Katie about the two of you.

'Mind you, *I* can't say too much,' Guy confessed. 'Chrissie and I fell in love virtually at first glance. Have you told Charlotte yet?'

'Er...no...she's away on a field trip at the moment,' Seb told him. Just what was going on...what the *hell* was Katie playing at? Was this some sort of crazy scheme she had dreamed up to punish him for kissing her, touching her...making it public that they were supposed to be a couple and then equally publicly dropping him? She was a Crighton after all, a member of a family who, historically, considered themselves to be a cut above everyone else, and *he* was a Cooke, a member of a family who equally historically had been considered to be the lowest of the low.

An hour later, when Guy dropped him off outside the house he was renting it was late evening. Unlocking the door Seb picked up the pile of mail off the mat.

He felt tired and irritated and in need of a shower, but more than any of that...

Taking the stairs two at a time he opened his bedroom door and quickly stripped off his clothes.

Florida had been hot and humid and he'd remained pretty much in the air-conditioned hotels, but the colour of his skin had still darkened slightly. He was naturally olive-skinned like Guy, and as he stood under the shower and soaped his body, the muscles in his arms and back stood out beneath his flesh.

While he towelled himself dry he replayed the messages on his answer machine. There was one from the interior designer telling him that the apartment was finished and ready for him to move into, as they had agreed.

Seb frowned as he reached out and switched off the machine. By rights what he ought to do if he had any sense was make himself a light supper and then go straight to bed. He was jet-lagged and in no mood to behave calmly or logically, so why, he asked himself sardonically half an hour later, if he knew that why was he right now in his car heading for the apartment, knowing that Katie had moved into hers?

He had every right to demand an explanation he justified to himself and he fully intended to do so.

Katie had had a very difficult day. One of her clients had been so late for his appointment with her she had had to go without any lunch break or even a cup of coffee in order to catch up, and then in the afternoon when she arrived in court, she had discovered that some of the papers she needed were missing and consequently she had been faced with the embarrassment of asking the judge for a postponement and that had not gone down well.

Add to that the fact that her car exhaust had disintegrated on the drive home from Chester and Katie felt it was no wonder that all she wanted was some peace and quiet and an early night.

She was soaking in the bath trying to relax the tension out of her shoulders when she heard the faint shrill of her intercom.

Cursing under her breath she climbed out of the bath, grabbing a towel on her way as she padded damply towards the intercom, flicking the switch and saying tiredly,

'Yes. Who is it?'

'Seb Cooke.'

Seb! Seb was *back*. Panic squeezed the breath out of her lungs, rendering her incapable of making any kind of verbal response.

'Katie.' Seb's voice was ominously charged with quiet fury.

'I was just on my way to bed,' she told him, not untruthfully, even while her conscience warned her that she was being a coward and that by far the most sensible and responsible thing to do was to see him and explain what had happened... Explain...! If only it was *that* easy.

She closed her eyes and then opened them again as she heard Seb saying softly,

'On your way to bed. Well, how very appropriate...in view of our...relationship...'

So he *had* heard. Not that she had doubted it, the very tone of his voice had told her that he knew.

Katie took a deep breath. There was nothing else for it. She was going to *have* to face him.

'I... I can explain,' she whispered into the intercom. 'But not now...tomorrow...'

'Now!' Seb returned implacably. 'Unless of course you want me to telephone your parents and inform them that their daughter is a...'

'No... No...now, then...' Katie agreed, momentarily forgetting that all she was wearing was a damp towel as she hurriedly activated the button to unlock the front door.

She froze as Seb walked in. There was a faint dark shadow along his jaw and he looked every bit as angry as he had sounded, but when he saw her, instead of unleashing the torrent of angry questions she had expected, he checked and looked at her very deliberately and lengthily.

Her face burned as Katie suddenly realised how he must be seeing her, her hair bunched up on top of her head, her body still damp from her bath, her only covering her soft cream towel.

'I... I'll just go and get dressed,' she heard herself stammering as her body reacted instantly and uncontrollably to the way he was looking at her, as instantly and uncontrollably as it had done when he had kissed her, touched her. Not that the heat burning her skin now had anything to do with her earlier apprehension or self-consciousness.

Mesmerised Katie stared right back into his eyes, her breathing suddenly laboured and shallow. A shocking surge of sexual heat shot through her veins. It must be the anxiety of the last few days that was having such a dangerous effect on her she told herself weakly. It must be because of that that she was experiencing this extraordinary reaction to Seb... that she was...

Dizzily she blinked but without being able to break

the intensity of his burning stare. What was happening to her? Why was she feeling her whole body trembling, aching with a need that seemed to have been conjured up out of nowhere, like a whirlwind, a tornado, ready to wreak total destruction on her?

'I... I can explain,' she told him huskily, and she didn't know herself whether she meant she could explain why everyone thought they were a couple or that she could explain why she was feeling the way she was, but instead of agreeing Seb simply walked towards her, telling her softly,

'Don't bother. I've changed my mind. It isn't an *explanation* I want...'

'It...it isn't...?'

Wide-eyed, Katie watched him, knowing instinctively what was going to happen but totally unable to respond in the way she knew she ought to be doing to her own danger. Instead of shock or fear or anger, what she was actually feeling was a roller-coaster surge of frantic excitement, of having stepped outside her normal cautious carefulness.

'No, it isn't...' Seb confirmed.

He was a hand span away from her now and as she walked back from him, her eyes never leaving his face, he followed her until she was backed up against the wall.

'Seb,' she protested shakily.

He had placed his palms flat against the wall either side of her, effectively imprisoning her.

'Apparently, it's common knowledge in Haslewich that you and I are...together,' he told her softly and quietly, spacing out every word so that she could feel the warmth of his breath against her skin. '...that we are...lovers...'

'No!' Katie protested. 'No...!'

'Yes,' Seb insisted. 'And since that's what supposedly we are—'

And then he lowered his head and kissed her with a mixture of passion and desire and infused anger that left her mute and helpless, his mouth burning hers as he refused to end the kiss, punishing her, savaging her with its angry heat.

And yet, beneath that anger, some age-old female wisdom told Katie that there was something else, relaying the information to her along all the most sensitive pathways of her body, tiny trickles of knowledge, awareness and emotion that together became a swift unstoppable flood of powerfully female response, as though independently of her brain, her senses knew *exactly* what to do, how to use Seb's passion to burn away his anger, leaving in its place a pure and almost unbearably intense fiery passion.

She had, Katie recognised dizzily, as her lips parted beneath the thrust of Seb's tongue, aroused him to the point where his need was a white-hot driven urgency blinding him to reality and tempting her, tormenting her, to give in to her own body's wild inner clamouring to respond to him with an equal lack of inhibition. After all, she was as human as any other woman, wasn't she? She was just as capable of experiencing sensual desire and longing, just as capable of needing to satisfy the ache deep down inside her own body, which was rapidly becoming an overriding, overwhelming, out of control force; a tumultuous flood of fiery, bitter-sweet urgency sweeping aside all obstacles in its path, all logic and reason, all thoughts that warned her that what was happening, that what she was contemplating, must not be allowed to happen.

What, after all, was she holding back for? Why was

she denying herself the sexual fulfilment that other women of her age took for granted. Why was she marooning herself on an isolated island of inexperience and self-conscious ignorance. Because she loved Gareth? Was she then to remain as she was all her life? Was she to remain untouched, unfulfilled...unknown by any man and unknowing of her own sexuality? Tonight, with Seb, she could experience all that she had previously denied herself. Tonight, with Seb, she could become fully a woman and fulfil her destiny. With Seb she could...

As her mind registered the dangers of her thoughts it rejected them instantly and totally, but her body seemed to have divorced itself completely from her brain, following a path of its own choosing, recklessly taking control. Her tongue touched Seb's, delicately sparring with it, a sharp shudder of reaction galvanising her body as Seb instantly responded to her silent encouragement. His hands left the wall and cupped her shoulders, his body hard against the softness of her own and so intimately close to it that she could feel, not just the fierce pounding of his heart but the far more intimate beat of his body pulse as well.

As though someone else had directed their movements, her arms reached out towards him, wrapping themselves around him while his hands moved urgently down over her body coming to rest against the round curves of her buttocks as he pulled her off the wall and even tighter into his intimate embrace.

Neither of them spoke. There was no need. Both of them knew what was happening, what was going to happen, and where the passage of arms between them to which Seb's passionate kiss was merely a prelude was leading.

When Seb shifted her body slightly in his arms, dragging his mouth from hers so that he could caress the soft flesh of her throat and then the curve of her naked shoulder, Katie made no move to stop him, and no move either to do anything to conceal from him the openly visible shudders of reaction coursing through her body. Her eyes open, silently she witnessed every touch of his hands, his mouth on her body, her expression registering every nuance of reaction and response she was feeling.

The heat of what was happening made her feel as though it was burning her up; as though she was being consumed, broken down, into the basic components of her essential self. And while a part of her was shocked by what was happening and by what she was doing, another recklessly urged her on.

There was a moment when, looking deep into her eyes, Seb slowly stood back from her, before reaching out to remove the towel from her body. She knew she should stop him, when she was helplessly and painfully aware of how very different this, her own first experience of male desire, would be from the tenderness and gentle joy her twin must have known with Gareth, a moment when she shivered and hesitated, but then some deep fierce inner force urged her on, drove her past that barrier. She was *not* Louise, and Gareth would *never* love her. She would *never* experience the gentle, tender warmth of his possession and so, instead, she must take this darker, deeper and far more dangerous pathway to sexual fulfilment.

Seb was still watching her as though waiting for her to do or say something. Katie looked at him. She had crossed her Rubicon and made up her mind. Very calmly she unfastened the towel herself and let it drop to the floor, her gaze on Seb's.

For a second she thought he wasn't going to move.

His eyes met and held hers without the involuntary betraying drop to her naked body she had expected, and then she saw the muscle twitch spasmodically in his jaw and that gave her the courage to let her gaze move very deliberately from his face to his body and to the tell-tale straining of the fabric of his trousers across his groin.

As though that one tiny glance had electrified him, Seb moved, closing the distance between them and sweeping her up in his arms.

The light from the two bedside lamps Katie had switched on before having her bath bathed the bedroom in a soft warm glow. The antique quilt Olivia had given her as a moving-in present lay across the foot of the bed, the heavy ivory damask curtains which had come from home covered the windows, enclosing the room and making it feel almost cocoon-like.

Katie had expected Seb to carry her over to the bed and immediately place her on it but instead, just short of it, he lowered her to her feet, gathering her up against the hard heat of his own body and then, bending his head to kiss her slowly at first and then, as his passion ignited, with a white-hot heat that made Katie feel as though the air surrounding them could self-combust. But even more shocking than Seb's fierce passion was her own response to it.

A long time ago in another life, another Katie would have been totally shocked at the wantonness—the *eagerness* with which *this* Katie pressed her naked body against Seb's fully clothed one, opening her mouth to his kiss just as fiercely and passionately eager for Seb to take the moistness, sweetness of her mouth, as Seb was to devour it. Their tongues met, meshed, stroked, caressed, tangling and entwining as erotically as they both knew their bodies would soon be doing, gliding against one another. Flesh to flesh, soft and smooth, hard and hot, each seeking out and fitting every curve and plane of the other.

In the distance Katie could hear a soft keening sound rising and falling as rhythmically as each thrust of Seb's tongue against her own, but she had no idea that she was the one making that sound. All she did know was that this was what she had been born for, this was something so fierce, so elemental, so necessary to her that she had no idea how she had ever lived without knowing it.

Seb had lifted one hand to cup her head while the other…

She shuddered deeply as it swept, stroked over her naked skin leaving in its wake a trail, a starburst of tiny fiery darts of aching pleasure, imposing on her body's memory a yearning, a hunger, to be touched that way again, and again…and again…

She wasn't even aware of speaking her need out loud until she felt Seb's hands sweep her body a second and a third time, both hands this time caressing her from the rounded ball of her shoulders right the way down to the equally rounded curve of her bottom and then back up again, the pads of his thumbs exquisitely abrasive against the sensitivity of her nipples.

This was what she had been made for, her whole body seemed to be singing with wild wanton pleasure as though somehow he had unearthed from deep within her a hitherto unknown chord of such strong sensuality and passion that the beat, the throb of it, was so powerful that it made her feel dizzy and faint.

Just to have Seb's thumbs brush lightly against her tight hard nipples exploded a sensation inside her like a flash fire, shocking, elemental, hot, out of control, an aching quivering life-force over which she had abso-

lutely no control, a need, an urge, that made her want
to reach for his hands and hold them against her breasts
to reach for his mouth and...

Sensations exploded deep in the pit of her belly and
Katie was lost. She no longer recognised the woman she
had become or the emotions and desires she was experiencing. What had happened to her longing for a quiet,
gentle, tender lover, a man who would treat her as
though she was as fragile as delicate porcelain, who
would woo her with gentle words and the lightest of
careful touches? What had happened to that inner fear
which had always made her recoil, even from the
thought of a sexual role for herself that wasn't completely passive and restrained? Never had she imagined
herself being capable of such sexual hunger, such sensual womanly aggression.

She closed her eyes on a deep shudder of intense reaction as Seb, without needing her to say what she
wanted, cupped her breasts and then lowered his head
towards them.

Even the warmth of his breath against her skin was
enough to make her tremble wildly in response and when
he opened his mouth and started to circle the hard point
of her nipple with the tip of his tongue Katie thought
she was going to faint with the violence of her own
reactions. Frantically she wound her fingers through
Seb's hair, urging him closer and closer to her breast
moaning out loud, begging for him to end her torment
and take the whole of her erect pulsating nipple into his
mouth and slowly suck the tormenting ache of desire
from it.

And yet, when he did so, instead of satisfying her and
stilling that hunger, it only seemed to increase it, feed
it, stoke it so that her hands were tugging at the fasten-

ings on his shirt, almost tearing the buttons from their button holes in her need to experience the reality of his flesh beneath her own fingertips.

Distantly she was aware of Seb helping her, of him removing his clothes at the same time as he continued to caress her, but the mechanics of what he was doing were lost on her as she whimpered in pleasure at the discovery of his naked flesh against the hands touching it, touching him with the blind hunger, the need of a starving person facing the most sumptuous banquet imaginable.

Seb's body was, she recognised dizzily, a feast for each and every one of her previously starved senses. Sight, sound, scent, touch…taste… She wanted to satisfy them all, to positively gorge herself on what she was being offered.

Vaguely Katie was aware that she ought to be shocked by what she was feeling, by how she was acting. Her whole behaviour was so totally unlike her, her needs were so unfamiliar to her, but there was no space, no time, no will within her to listen to any unwanted warning voices. This was the real her. She felt as though she was a chrysalis shedding its restrictive coat to emerge for the first time with the freedom to be as she really was.

As Seb placed her on the bed she reached up and kissed his shoulder, closing her eyes in open appreciation as she breathed in the heated aroused scent of his body, tasted it on her tongue.

'You feel so good,' she whispered huskily to him, the words tumbling from her lips in the brief spaces of time she could allow in her eager oral exploration of his body. 'You smell so good… You taste so good…'

Her words seemed to snap the final cords binding

Seb's self-control. Katie heard him groan, a low exciting growl of sound that sent actual physical shock waves of sensation racing over her own skin and then he was holding her, lifting her, positioning her so that every part of her body was open to the intimate caress of his hands and mouth. The sensation of him touching her, caressing her, leaving her with the moist heat of his tongue, sending wave after wave of arousal crashing down over her until she was drowning in her own longing and need for his full possession.

There was no time for her to feel apprehension or even hesitation, only a growing vortex of need that drew her into the maelstrom of its tumultuous heart, the only sound she could hear the thud of Seb's heartbeat and the sobbing cry of her own piercing longing.

There was no sense of shock or pain, only the intensity of her own longing, her own urgency. That, and her awed comprehension of how perfectly they fit together, of how dizzyingly strong her own sensual reaction to him was. He moved and she moved with him, their bodies in perfect harmony, creating between them a rhythm that echoed the life force of the universe itself, so completely at one with one another, so perfectly complementing one another that Katie felt as though she was being buoyed up, swept along, carried by a force as pure and spiritual as it was sensual and earthly.

What was happening for her was so sublimely perfect that she felt as though not just her body, but her mind, her heart, her whole being had entered another dimension. Awash with the waves of sensation that had crashed through her, carrying her over that final barrier and safely into the calm place that was the other side of the chasm she had crossed, she reached out to Seb, touching his throat with questing fingers, the smile she gave him beneath her suddenly too heavy eyelids, soft and womanly, full of knowledge and fulfilment.

Seb though wasn't returning her smile. His eyes were dark and unreadable, his face set and something close to anger breaking through the quietly controlled pitch of his voice as he demanded,

'Why didn't you tell me...*warn* me?'

Self-consciously, Katie looked away from him, her euphoria disappearing at the cold disapproval of his voice.

'It was your first time, wasn't it?' Seb was demanding sharply as she looked away from him unable to hold or endure the searching look he was focusing on her.

There wasn't any point in denying the truth, not when he had so obviously realised.

'Yes. It was,' Katie agreed calmly.

She heard Seb curse under his breath and winced at the anger she could hear.

'You should have *told* me, and...'

'...and what?' Katie found the courage to question, her own lips only trembling very slightly as she twisted them into a wry smile. 'You'd have stopped?'

She saw from the dark surge of colour burning up under his skin that Seb knew what she meant. *He* had been as incapable of stopping as *she* had been of drawing his attention to her virginity.

'*Why* should I have told you?' she asked him and then looking at him she said simply, 'It...it couldn't have been any...any better and I...'

Seb cursed again.

'You were a *virgin*,' he reminded her furiously, 'and I...'

'You made love to me as though I were a woman and

not a girl,' Katie suggested. Pride darkened her eyes, her head lifting as she spoke to him.

'Perhaps I *didn't* tell you because I *wanted* to be treated as a woman…an equal…'

'No…you're lying,' Seb denied sharply. 'No woman of your intelligence and your age waits so long without having a purpose, a reason for doing so, and certainly a woman like you would *never* allow such an important rite of passage to be… No…you must have been waiting for something or someone…'

He was so close to the truth that Katie held her breath praying inwardly that Seb wouldn't inadvertently stumble on it and realise…

Realise what? That she had dreamed up for herself a totally false image of her own sexuality? That she had spent years fantasising about a sexual experience and a man so far removed from the reality of what her body had told her tonight it really wanted, that the enormity of the gulf between what *she* had believed she *had* wanted and what in fact she really *had* wanted was so huge that even now she could barely grasp how wrong she had been?

The person she had believed she was before tonight could never have felt, wanted, needed, *enjoyed* what she had just experienced with Seb. By rights she knew she ought to feel, at best self-conscious and at worst downright ashamed of what she had done and why she had done it, and certainly it was something she couldn't envisage ever discussing even with someone so close to her as her twin.

How on earth would Louise react if she were to tell her that she had been so overwhelmed by her own sexual longings that she had practically begged Seb, a man she knew she didn't love, but who in that mad moment of

intensity she had wanted with an urgency and despera-
tion far stronger than anything she had ever previously
experienced, to take her, possess her, fill and complete
her?

She had, she recognised on a shocking surge of self-
realisation, wanted exactly what had happened and
worse, she had wanted it to be with Seb who she knew
didn't love her and who she knew was just about as
different from Gareth as it was possible for a man to be.

'Why?' Seb was asking her tersely. 'Why now? Why
me?'

He reached out, taking hold of her by her shoulders,
dragging her upright to face him before she could stop
him.

'What's going on, Katie? I arrive home to discover
that you and I are supposedly having a relationship, that
we are effectively *already* a couple, although you and I
both know that that just isn't so...or rather it wasn't,'
he corrected himself grimly.

'*That* was an accident,' Katie told him immediately.
'I never...' She stopped, biting her lip and then wincing
as the touch of her teeth against its tenderness reminded
her of the intimacy of the kisses they had shared. Her
face flushed a soft rosy pink as she tried to wriggle free
of him and another part of her body reminded her even
more insistently of just how intimate that intimacy had
been.

'An accident?'

'Yes,' she insisted. 'Louise jumped to the wrong con-
clusions about... about us...I...'

She stopped. How could she explain just why she
hadn't totally and immediately corrected her twin. 'I
tried to tell her, but it...it wasn't easy...' She hung her
head. 'She feels uncomfortable with me sometimes,

guilty almost because she's…because she has Gareth and their life together and it's hard to make her understand that I'm happy as I am.'

'She wants you to be like her, part of a couple—settled…' Seb interrupted her, adding intuitively, 'And so it was easier to allow her to think that her assumptions were correct.'

'Yes. Yes, it was,' Katie agreed. 'I never dreamed that she would tell anyone else or that…'

She stopped and shook her head. 'I couldn't believe it when my mother started talking to me about you…about us, as though… I should have admitted the truth then, I wanted to… I knew how angry you'd be once you got to hear about it.'

'I *was* angry,' Seb admitted brusquely. 'But that's no excuse for what I did… Why didn't you stop me…tell me?'

'Perhaps I didn't want to,' Katie told him honestly, her eyes clouding a little with the pain of her private thoughts.

She wasn't being totally honest with him. Katie knew that. She hadn't told him the truth about why she had allowed Louise to believe they were involved with one another. But how could she tell him without exposing herself to even more humiliation and, anyway, how could she tell anyone else about her feelings for Gareth when she hadn't told her twin? And now, if she told him about Gareth, could she then go on to admit that, despite the longevity of her love, despite what she had believed to be the strength and permanence of it, the moment Seb had touched her she had been overwhelmed by such a compulsive urgency, such a white-hot burn of desire that it simply hadn't been possible for her to think of anything or anyone else?

She gave him a direct look and said quietly and rue-fully, her mouth curving in a semi-self-mocking smile,

'Perhaps I was beginning to feel that my virginity was getting dangerously close to the end of its shelf-life. But I wanted you Seb... I can't explain why or how and I wasn't even thinking about my virginity, I wasn't ca-pable of that kind of logic, of any kind of reasonable thinking... I can't explain why or what... I just...'

She stopped, her eyes momentarily shining with emo-tional tears as she admitted with painful honesty,

'Yes, perhaps I *should* have warned you...told you...or stopped you...but...'

'But...' Seb prompted her when she fell silent and bowed her head so that all he could see was the top of it.

'...but I didn't want to,' Katie repeated huskily as she lifted her head to meet his gaze. 'I had no idea that sex could be so...so...'

'...so dangerous,' Seb offered sardonically.

'So *total*,' Katie amended as she added bravely, 'I'm not going to allow myself to feel guilty or ashamed about what happened or about the way I felt, Seb. I...it was...it was wonderful,' she told him recklessly, the words little more than a shy whisper of sound as her face grew pink and she looked away from him.

'*Wonderful*!' Seb repeated explosively. 'Have you *any* idea! None of this should have happened. None of it. You and I...'

'...don't even like one another. I know...' Katie agreed sadly. 'Maybe that's the way passion is, I don't know. Perhaps you would be able to say better than me.'

'You think so?' Seb shook his head. 'What just hap-pened between us was as much of a ''first time'' for me as it was for you. I don't make a habit of allowing myself to lose control like that and I certainly don't enjoy knowing that...'

He stopped, shaking his head while Katie suggested practically, 'Well, at least no one other than ourselves need ever know about it. Tomorrow I'll explain to my mother that Louise got it wrong and...'

She tensed as Seb suddenly moved abruptly away from her pulling the disarranged bedclothes over his lower body.

His rejection of her and his patent lack of interest in what she was saying hurt her more than she liked having to recognise and the warmth and happiness that had followed their lovemaking was quickly being replaced by a sense of loss and loneliness.

'If you want...' she began stiffly and then she saw the way he was looking at her body and she knew immediately and exactly just what it was he did want and her face burned bright scarlet with a heart-stopping mixture of shock and excitement.

Excitement because Seb still wanted her, because the reason he had reached for those concealing covers was because his body was reacting to the proximity of hers, because...

Before she could stop herself or even think critically or sensibly about what she was doing she heard herself whispering softly, 'Seb, please stay with me tonight...*all* night...'

'Stay with you...'

His voice was slurred and gruff as though his throat was hurting him somehow. Fascinated Katie watched as he closed his eyes and swallowed, her whole body shivering in mute reactive awareness of the strong tide of need which was already building to threaten their defences.

'Yes. I want you to,' she told him. 'I want you…' She gave him a brief look full of female knowledge as she reminded him, 'After all, I'm not a virgin anymore now.'

She could see the heat leaping in his eyes as immediately and dangerously as though she had thrown a lighted match onto petrol. When he reached for her his skin felt like hot satin and when she touched him he cried out, suffering the eager exploration of her hands and then her mouth until his whole body was racked by seismic shudders of uncontrollable reaction.

'Stay with me' she had begged him and he did, through the tumult of her own hungry desire and beyond it, holding her through the night as she slept.

What the hell was happening to him? Seb asked himself defeatedly. He had come to see her tonight intent only on demanding an explanation from her, furiously angry with her and now… He looked down at where she slept in his arms. Now he knew that ridiculously, illogically, he never ever wanted to let her go.

'Stay with me' she had asked and in doing so he had somehow rewritten all the rules he had laid down for the way he intended to live his life.

CHAPTER EIGHT

'COFFEE...'

Sleepily Katie opened her eyes and then sat bolt upright in her bed as she saw Seb standing in the doorway to her bedroom, fully dressed and holding a mug of fragrantly scented coffee.

Wide-eyed, she watched him as he walked towards her without waiting for her response. Less than a handful of hours ago, as the dawn had started to lighten the sky, she had woken him from his sleep whispering to him that she wanted him. She blushed now to recall just how wantonly insistent she had been and just how femininely persuasive as she had eagerly caressed his body. Not that he had needed very much persuasion. She winced as she moved and felt her own body's sharp response to the intensity of the long hours of lovemaking they had shared.

'You don't have to stay now,' she told him huskily as she took the mug of coffee from him and avoided looking into his eyes. 'You must want to get back to your own place...you must have things to do...'

'Well yes,' he agreed, informing her laconically, 'I do have some telephone calls to make and I shall certainly need a change of clothes before we meet your parents for lunch. Your mother called.'

'*What*?' Katie sat bolt upright in bed.

'She rang earlier while you were still asleep. I answered the phone,' Seb told her matter-of-factly.

Katie stared at him as though she couldn't believe what she was hearing.

'My mother rang and *you* answered the phone?'

'Mmm…' Seb agreed.

'What did she say? What did you say?' Katie began wildly. 'Oh, but this is awful. Now she's never going to believe that you and I aren't…'

'That you and I aren't what?' Seb asked her ironically. 'That you and I aren't lovers…but we are!'

Nonplussed Katie looked at him.

'But that was private,' she told him huskily when she eventually found her voice. 'It was…' She stopped.

'It was what?' Seb probed, but Katie shook her head. How could she tell him that what they had shared, what she had experienced was for her, even in the sharp clear light of morning—even knowing logically what she did know—something so special…so mystical, that she knew that even if she could she would not have changed a single heartbeat of it?

Every thought, every image she had ever had with Gareth as her lover had been completely extinguished by the heat of Seb's passion, extinguished and obliterated.

'None of this should be happening,' Katie told him helplessly. 'You shouldn't… You don't… My parents think we're a couple, but we're not…'

'No,' Seb agreed, 'but then I could hardly tell your mother that when she telephoned and learned that I was here, could I? What would I have said? Yes, I've spent the night in bed with Katie but that was all it was…just a night in bed…'

Katie's face drained of colour as she listened to him. If they knew the truth her parents would be so shocked, so shamed by her behaviour.

As he watched the emotions chase one another across her mobile face, Seb reflected inwardly that he was going to be in big trouble if she found out that *he* was the one who had suggested to her mother that they should all meet for lunch and that *he* was the one who, by the tone of his voice and the careful words he had used, had made it clear to Jenny Crighton that he and Katie had spent the night together, rather than her assuming it.

Tradition might have it that it was the woman who trapped the man into a relationship with sex and not the other way around, but last night had proved to him, if he had needed any proof, just how unreliable tradition actually was. Katie might have been a virgin but there had been no shrinking hesitancy, no fear or apprehension, no holding back or coyness in the way she had responded to him, the way she had *given* to him.

Early that morning, while she had slept, he had gone for a solitary walk along the river needing the time alone to make sense out of the jumble of thoughts and emotions jostling for supremacy inside him.

As he had walked he had admitted that he would be a fool to pretend that he had not known even before last night, just how strong and dangerous his feelings for her actually were. You simply didn't get so hyped up and angry about a person who didn't matter, and *he* certainly wouldn't have had the kind of physical reactions he had had last night without... As he paused to watch a pair of swans with their offspring he had been forced to recognise a truth he had been hiding from himself all along.

Right from the very start, the very first time he had seen her, Katie had had a profound effect on him. The anger, the intensity he had experienced that very first time he had seen her had been too strong, too alien to his normal behaviour pattern. It was as though at some deep-seated buried level his senses had locked on to her, reacted to her, and he had suppressed that reaction. What was he trying to say to himself, that he had fallen in love with her and then gone into denial?

Well, he certainly hadn't been in any kind of denial last night, had he? he had mocked himself.

As he had watched the swans he had acknowledged that while he might love Katie, she most certainly did *not* love him.

No, but she *wanted* him. His body had quickened fiercely and hungrily in response to this thought and his need to turn round and go straight back to rouse her from her sleep and take her in his arms had been so strong that the effort of controlling it had made him grunt out loud in protest at his own pain.

As he walked back towards the house, he was ironically aware of how the whole of his life had come full circle. He and Sandra had married, confusing their physical desire for one another with love, but now that he had actually come face to face with the real thing, now that he actually *knew* love, he could see so plainly the world of difference that separated what he had felt then with what he felt now. But if he had made the mistake of committing himself to a relationship based on physical desire once he wasn't about to do so again. Katie deserved better. She deserved not just to be loved, and he most certainly *did* love her, but to know love, to feel it, experience it, share it for herself.

He had walked back into her apartment fully intending to make it plain to her that he had no expectations, that what had happened was an isolated incident, over and done with, when the phone had rung and he had answered it and without even knowing himself what he was going to do he had subtly confirmed to her mother that they were lovers, trapping Katie in her family's expectations and his own love. He was old enough to have known better, old enough to have *done* better by his love and by Katie herself.

'This can't be happening,' Katie was whispering plaintively as she nursed the now cold mug of coffee he had brought her. Perhaps it shouldn't be happening, but it quite definitely was and contrary to her expectations, instead of accusing her of messing up both their lives, Seb seemed to be totally relaxed about the whole situation.

'*I* wasn't the one who started it,' Seb reminded her wryly.

Katie frowned. No he wasn't and she had only herself to blame for the situation she now found herself in—and in more ways than one.

'I'll ring my mother and cancel lunch,' she told Seb quickly but, instead of greeting her suggestion with approval, an expression she found hard to define crossed his face then he shrugged and told her curtly,

'If you wish.'

Ten minutes later when he had left to return home Katie decided that she couldn't fathom him out at all. But was she any more capable of understanding *herself* than she was him? Last night her behaviour had been completely out of character. So much so, that even though she was now on her own she still blushed to recall some of the things she had said—and done!

She telephoned her mother as soon as she had showered, explaining with her fingers crossed behind her back that Seb wasn't going to be able to make it for lunch as he had realised he had some work he had to attend to urgently.

'In fact,' she began, taking a deep breath, suddenly determined not to end the telephone call until she had told her mother the truth, but before she could do so her mother was saying quickly, 'Darling, I have to go, there's someone at the door. Never mind about lunch, we'll fix something for another day, and besides,' she laughed gently, 'I'm sure that you and Seb would much prefer to be on your own…'

She would certainly like to be on her own Katie admitted, completely and *totally* on her own. Dressing quickly she picked up her bag and her car keys. She needed time to think, time to let the reality of what had happened sink in fully.

While Katie was hurrying down to her car, Seb was getting out of the shower. As he padded naked across his bedroom he caught sight of Charlotte's photograph. She had been telling him with increasing insistence that it was time he fell in love and remarried. She had taken an immediate liking to Katie. Look at the way she had reacted to that gypsy girl's ridiculous prediction. Seb froze and closed his eyes, muttering a pious prayer-cum-plea beneath his breath as he suddenly remembered what, in the heat of last night's passion, he had so recklessly forgotten.

He knew he had a clean bill of health so what they had done, while irresponsible, was not hazardous, but from the point of view of potential conception… There were modern methods, though. Safeguards… As he hurried towards the door the telephone rang. He hesitated and paused and then quickly reached for the receiver, his heart starting to thud with anxiety as the leader of the field trip Charlotte had been attending the past week explained that there had been a small mishap and that she had suffered a fall.

'They're keeping her in hospital to check that she isn't suffering from concussion,' he explained to Seb, 'but I can assure you that there's nothing for you to worry about.'

'Where is she? Which hospital?' was Seb's uncompromising response.

Before he left he telephoned Katie's flat, waiting for her to answer for several minutes before hanging up. He couldn't delay any more, not with Charlotte in hospital. He would have to ring Katie later on his mobile and warn her of the danger he had left her exposed to.

Later, Katie couldn't explain, even to herself, what had prompted her to do what she did or quite how or why she was on her way, virtually at a moment's notice, to Brussels. She'd made a brief telephone call to her twin to warn her that she was coming, and another and even more muddled one to her mother, disjointedly explaining that she was at the airport and on her way to her sister and that she didn't know how long she would be gone. 'It will only be for a couple of days,' she reassured Jenny. 'Tell Dad and Livvy that I'm sorry to spring this on them, but...'

On the other end of the line Jenny simply listened. It was totally unlike Katie to behave so impulsively, but she couldn't help but be glad that the rift she had seen slowly growing between the two girls was now being mended. If Katie needed her twin enough to drop everything to fly over to her then Jenny knew that Louise would be there for her.

'She's gone where?' Jon demanded in astonishment when Jenny broke the news to him of Katie's unplanned visit to her twin sister.

'It will only be for a few days. It's just a short break,'

Jenny soothed him while he sighed in exasperation and then smiled ruefully at her.

'I certainly hope so. We're hellishly busy at the moment. What on earth brought this on?'

When Jenny simply looked at him he gave another rueful paternal sigh and guessed.

'Love trouble!'

'A small crisis of confidence I suspect,' Jenny told him.

'In *Seb*?' Jon frowned. He might not be either a possessive father nor the type who became vehemently verbally proactive on behalf of his children—right or wrong—but he was nevertheless *very* protective of them.

'If that's the case then I should have thought she'd be better off without him.'

'No, not in Seb,' Jenny told him gently. 'I suspect that the confidence she lacks is in herself... I noticed particularly how when she was at university she developed the habit of standing in the shadows as it were, of accepting second place...second best...'

'Like father—like daughter,' Jon offered ruefully as he and Jenny exchanged mutually understanding and loving looks. For many years Jon himself had stood in the shadow of his twin, so much so that his resultant lack of self-esteem had affected every aspect of his life and he and Jenny had been determined that their twin girls would not suffer similarly; encouraging them both to develop and be proud of their differences as well as their similarities.

'Seb will be good for her. He won't allow her to take a back seat in life. As a Cooke he'll know just what it means to sometimes have to fight to win other people's respect and, even more importantly, to maintain one's own. He will understand Katie's vulnerabilities and she'll see through his outer image of toughness to the sensitivity that lies beneath it.'

'Mmm...well, it all sounds very positive and hopeful.'

'I can see a very happy future ahead for the two of them.'

'And I can see a very expensive one ahead for us,' Jon riposted. 'Why couldn't fate have arranged for them to meet a little earlier? That way she and Louise could have had a double wedding, two for the cost of one, so to speak.'

The airport was exceptionally busy. After she had gone through to the departure lounge Katie checked the board for her flight and then made her way through the crowd to the coffee shop. As she did so, out of the corner of her eye she glimpsed a tall dark-haired man crossing the concourse in front of her.

Immediately a fierce surge of joy and excitement raced through her.

'Seb.'

His name was on her lips, her heart pounding. He was here. He had come to look for her. He *wanted* her. He *loved* her just as she loved him. She loved him! She loved Seb. For a few seconds Katie stood perfectly still as the world kaleidoscoped around her and the revelation of her own emotions hit her with all the devastating effect of a strong drug taking over her senses, entering her bloodstream. Her thoughts, her emotions were so searingly intense that she was oblivious to everything else going on around her. She might have been standing completely alone so little did the busy crowds around her impinge on her awareness.

She *loved* Seb.

She closed her eyes and said his name slowly, savouring it and then opened them again frantically searching for his familiar figure. But as she started to hurry towards him, he stopped and turned and with a sickening jolt Katie recognised that the man she had been following wasn't Seb at all and that now she had seen it she saw that his face bore no resemblance to Seb whatsoever. His features lacked the patrician nobility of Seb's. His bone structure was nowhere near as masculine, his eyes nothing like Seb's cool grey ones. He was quite simply not Seb and how on earth she had ever believed that he was, she couldn't imagine. Why, after all, would Seb be here? He didn't even *know* she was at the airport. He didn't know and would probably not have cared if he had. He certainly wouldn't have cared enough to come rushing here after her, to take her in his arms and declare undying love for her.

Seb love her?

This must be what the intense intimacy of the kind of sex they had shared did to a woman Katie decided, shivering almost feverishly. It made her vulnerable. It made her love the man who had shown her…given her such pleasure. Slowly Katie shook her head trying to clear the miasma of painful thoughts crowding into it.

Had she fallen in love with Seb when they had been making love or had she perhaps, unknown to herself, been attracted to him *before* that? She didn't know and had no way of ever knowing, but what she *did* know was that that moment, that split second of time when she had thought she had seen Seb, when she had believed he loved her, would be engraved on her heart and her memory for the rest of her life. There was no going back now from the discovery she had made or going back from the knowledge she had gained. No, there was no going back from *anything* now.

Absently Katie glanced at the departure board and then realised that they were boarding her flight. Like an automaton she made her way to the appropriate gate. *Now* she knew why she had felt so impelled to be with Louise, why she was being urged to seek out the one person who could help her to make sense out of what was happening to her. People didn't fall in love without knowing they had done so...did they? It just wasn't possible—was it? How *could* she have loved Seb without knowing that she did so?

Once on the plane Katie took her seat like a sleepwalker. Her mind, her heart, *all* of her was filled with images and thoughts of Seb. Seb striding angrily into her apartment. Seb kissing her with such furious passion. Seb touching her body; looking at her, his anger transmuted into pure molten desire. Seb...

Why hadn't she had some inkling, some suspicion, some built-in protective warning system to tell her that this would happen; that she would feel like this—*love* like this?

'Katie...over here...'

Automatically Katie turned in the direction she could hear her twin's voice coming from. Louise was waiting for her on the other side of the flight gate. Quickly Katie hurried towards her, all the things she had planned to say; the logical explanations she had intended to make, forgotten as they rushed into one another's arms.

Tears filled her eyes, rolling down her face as she told Louise chokily, 'Lou, I'm in love...with Seb...'

Releasing her Louise studied her and then asked gently, 'Is that a problem? I thought the two of you made a good couple.'

'Us being a couple isn't the problem,' Katie admitted.

'Or rather… Where's Nick?' she asked, changing the subject and looking round for Louise's little boy.

'With Gareth,' Louise told her promptly. 'Gareth had a few days' leave owing and so I told him it was time that he and Nick did a little bit of father and son bonding. They've gone to stay with friends for a few days.'

There was no way that Louise was going to tell her twin that until she had received her phone call she *too* had been planning to take part in this short family break. Gareth had raised his eyebrows but made no demure when she had told him that there had been a change of plan.

'Katie *never* asks for anything,' Louise had told him soberly. 'Of the two of us *I'm* always the one who makes demands on her. She needs me Gareth. I have to be here for her. I owe it to her,' she had finished softly.

Now, as she looked at her twin's pale face, Louise knew that she had been right to listen to that small inner voice.

'Come on,' she announced, taking hold of Katie's arm. 'You and I are going to go and have a proper girlie lunch. There's this fabulous restaurant we've discovered not far away from the house.'

Katie started to protest and shake her head. The last thing she felt like doing was eating, but typically Louise wasn't giving her the opportunity to object, tucking her arm through Katie's and urging her towards the exit.

As Seb drove towards the Yorkshire Dales, the site of Charlotte's field trip, a sudden bottle-neck in the traffic slowed him down enough that he had the opportunity to reach for his mobile phone and punch in Katie's number. He had made a mental note of it earlier in the morning while he had been on the phone to her mother, never guessing how soon he was going to need to use it.

Impatiently he waited as the phone rang, willing Katie to pick up the receiver, smothering the sense of anguish and disappointment he felt when there was no reply. Charlotte had been taken to the hospital nearest to the field trip site and although Seb had spoken to the staff nurse in charge of her ward and had been reassured that keeping her in was only a precaution and that she was fine, he knew his natural parental fears would not be allayed until he had seen her.

He just hoped that he would be able to reach Katie by telephone before too long. If he couldn't... 'You'll have a boy child' the gypsy had said. A child...a boy...a son... Katie's son... There was no way he was going to abdicate his parental responsibilities a *second* time. No way he was going to be an absent father. No way he was not going to be fully and totally a part of his child's life...

Charlotte had been lucky... He had been lucky in that his absence had not damaged her, but he still had to carry the guilt of knowing he had not been there for her when he ought to have been, he still had to bear the guilt of knowing that his own selfish behaviour could have compromised her happiness and her life... Just as his own selfish behaviour could have resulted in the conception of another child.

Unplanned this baby may be, he acknowledged, but not unwanted. The sensation that had ripped through him at the thought of Katie carrying his child had shocked him. Charlotte was his daughter and he loved her, but he had never once felt anything for Sandra like he had just experienced now thinking about Katie conceiving and carrying his child.

He liked Sandra as a person, respected and admired her as a mother and as a wife—someone else's wife—but he didn't love her, had never loved her the way he did Katie. But Katie didn't love him and if she should have conceived because of his lack of self-control... God, what a mess he had made of everything.

'Truthfully, Louise, I'm just not hungry,' Katie protested. 'All I want...' A single, solitary tear slid down her face causing Louise to change her plans and the direction in which she was driving.

'What are you doing?' Katie protested in alarm as her twin did an illegal U-turn virtually in the middle of the busy city street.

'Don't worry,' Louise grinned. 'No one was watching... We're going home,' she added by way of explanation. 'We can talk properly there.'

The house Louise and Gareth were renting in Brussels was down a pretty, leafy road; a small town house with a good-sized, private rear garden.

'Come on,' Louise smiled reassuringly at her twin as she parked her car and then got out, walking round to the passenger door and waiting for Katie and then taking hold of her hand almost as though she thought she might run away, Katie acknowledged wearily.

But where, after all, was there for her to run to? *Who* was there for her to run to? Nowhere and no one. She just wished she hadn't made that ridiculously overemotional statement at the airport. No wonder Louise was treating her as though she had less common sense than her small son Nick.

'We'll sit out in the garden,' Louise announced as she led the way into the house and then through it out onto

a pretty paved patio area, virtually pushing Katie into
one of the comfortable garden chairs before telling her,

'Stay there. I'll go and get some wine...'

'I don't...' Katie began but Louise shook her head
and told her ruefully,

'Well *I* certainly do. Just one glass,' she suggested in
a more gentle voice. 'It will do you good.'

The wine Louise poured for them both was clean and
crisp and deliciously cold. It tasted good, Katie admitted,
shaking her head over the plate of sandwiches Louise
was offering her.

'So...tell me *everything*,' Louise commanded her.
'You're in love with Seb. Well, I could see that. What's
troubling you? Is it the thought of making such a big
commitment...marriage can seem very scary. I know.'

'No. It's nothing like that,' Katie interrupted her, taking a deep breath before saying starkly,

'What I let you think before, what I told you, simply
wasn't true. Not then... Seb and I weren't...hadn't...
There was *nothing* between us and...'

'But there is now,' Louise cut across Katie's stum-
bling explanations. 'Now you're in love with him...'

'Yes...' Katie looked down at her almost empty wine
glass feeling her face grow hot as certain memories
flooded through her. Then she drained the last of her
wine and turned to face Louise, telling her with a blunt-
ness that ordinarily would have been totally out of character for her, 'It... I... I went to bed with him. We had
sex...and it was...' She paused, her face growing even
hotter, but when she searched Louise's face and could
see no hint of shock or criticism there she took another
deep breath and continued, 'It was wonderful. I hadn't...
I never thought... He was angry at first. Angry with me
because he'd discovered that people were talking about

us as a couple. I tried to explain and apologise, but...he took hold of me and started to kiss me and then what had started out as... I couldn't help myself... I just wanted him so much,' Katie confessed in a low voice.

'I'd never imagined *I* could feel like that. Not me. My own feelings just overwhelmed me... I just wanted him so much. I know this must be hard for you to understand,' she told Louise, unable to fully look at her now. 'You and Gareth...you love one another and...'

'I didn't love him the first time I had sex with him,' Louise interrupted her to tell her matter of factly. 'Actually...' She stopped. 'Perhaps we're even more alike than either of us has ever recognised. Gareth was very angry with *me* the first time *we* made love, Katie, and I felt just the same as you've said you felt. *I* was the one who drove things on, who insisted...who seduced...' she underlined ruefully.

Katie lifted her head and listened warily.

'The first time I went to bed with Gareth I was convinced it was Saul I loved, not him. I was furiously angry with Gareth and with myself and he was equally furiously angry with me, but somehow all that anger became transmuted, transformed into something else.'

Katie closed her eyes and then opened them again.

'When I went to bed with Seb,' she confessed gruffly, 'I thought...' She stopped and bit her lip and then, looking right at her twin, she confessed huskily, 'I thought...felt...believed that it was really Gareth I loved.'

For a moment the silence between them was so intense, so profound, that Katie feared that she had gone too far, said too much, violated their twinship so severely that their lifelong bond had been severed, but then Louise moved, pushing back her chair, coming towards her, taking hold of her and hugging her so hard that Katie had to gasp for breath.

'Oh Katie, Katie, it's so awesome that we should both have experienced the same thing, that we should both have shared almost exactly the same things. You *know* what this means, don't you?' Louise demanded in a portentous voice.

Katie looked at her, her heart starting to beat heavily and painfully. What was Louise going to say? That because Katie had admitted to having loved Gareth things could never now be the same between them, that Louise could never again trust her...?

'No...what does it mean?' Katie forced herself to ask.

'It means that you and Seb are quite definitely meant for one another,' Louise told her excitedly. 'Just like Gareth and I were...'

Katie hated to disillusion her but she had to. Sadly she shook her head.

'No. Seb doesn't love me,' she told her positively.

'He took you to bed, made love to you,' Louise reminded her.

'He *wanted* me,' Katie agreed. 'But he doesn't *love* me,' she said painfully. She hesitated and then looked uncertainly at Louise.

'You won't say anything to Gareth about...about me having thought I loved him, will you?' she begged Louise. 'I realise now that...' She stopped. Even if she hadn't already recognised how unreal and unsupportable her supposed love for Gareth had really been, she knew that hearing Louise describe his anger with her when they had made love, and recognising that Gareth was the tender almost detached gentle lover she had imagined was nothing more than an unreal fantasy would have destroyed the fragile romantic image she had built up around her brother-in-law.

She had believed she loved him because there had been no one else there in her life for her *to* love, she realised with sudden wisdom. Loving Gareth had been a subtle form of emotional protection, of safeguarding her emotions. Rather like that thicket of briars which had grown up around Sleeping Beauty, and like the prince who had hacked his way through that thicket, Seb had found a way through *her* emotional protection and into her heart.

If she had gained nothing else from what had happened, she had at least gained maturity and a much deeper knowledge of her real self. And of course, she had regained the special closeness with Louise her twin.

An hour later as they strolled together through Brussels' shopping area, Katie paused to study the display in a small boutique window.

The dress, a cobwebby knit creation that clung lovingly and seductively to every curve of the mannequin's body was both impossibly expensive and even more impossibly provocative.

'He'll be furious with you for wearing it in public where other men's eyes could see what he wants to keep only for himself,' Louise murmured to her before adding temptingly, 'Why don't you buy it?'

'Certainly not,' Katie demurred. 'Have you seen the price, and besides where would I wear it? Mind you I could do with something,' she admitted ruefully. 'There's Gramps's "do" coming up...'

Louise rolled her eyes expressively and groaned, 'Don't remind me,' and then, as her voice changed tone and became quieter, she asked gently,

'What will you do?'

'…about Seb?' Katie responded. 'I don't know. Perhaps I should look for another job…move away…'

'Why not move here?' Louise suggested promptly. 'You'd get a job easily enough and we've got plenty of spare bedrooms… Or,' she added, pausing and then looking at Katie before saying firmly,

'You *could* always tell him how you feel, and then he…'

'No! That's impossible,' Katie denied immediately.

Ten minutes later while they were sitting in a café drinking coffee, Louise suddenly gave a small exclamation and got up. 'I've just remembered, I didn't put enough money in the parking ticket machine. You wait there while I go and get another ticket. I shan't be long…'

'No,' she insisted when Katie started to get up. 'There's no need for you to come. Finish your coffee and order us both a second cup… You don't know what a treat…a luxury…it is for me to simply be able to sit and drink coffee. I love Nick to pieces but just occasionally it's absolute bliss to have some time to myself. When you and Seb have that baby of yours you'll understand what I mean,' she added wickedly before hurrying down the street.

'*Dad*! What are *you* doing here?'

Seb grimaced as Charlotte came bounding into the foyer to the ward stopping dead as she saw him. He had arrived at the hospital ten minutes earlier and had just reached the ward where Charlotte had been hospitalised.

'What do you think?' he responded grimly.

'You came because of *me*?' Charlotte shook her head. 'But I'm fine, I promise. In fact I've just been discharged. Heaven knows why they insisted on keeping me in here.'

'You had a bad fall,' Seb pointed out curtly.

Charlotte rolled her eyes protestingly.

'I had a bit of a tumble,' she corrected him. 'Hardly a fall at all and if I hadn't bumped my head I doubt there would have been any of this silly panic. Heavens, if I'd been rushed off to hospital every time I fell over when I was growing up I'd have spent half my life there. Mum always used to complain that it must be the Cooke gene that made me so clumsy and so addicted to danger. According to her, *she* never so much as sustained the smallest scratch when she was growing up. I suppose I was a bit of a tomboy,' Charlotte allowed ruefully, a huge smile dimpling her face as she slid her arm through Seb's and teased him, 'You're going to have to get used to visits like this if you and Katie have that baby boy. No,' she corrected herself firmly, '*When* you have him... How *is* Katie by the way, is she here with you?'

Here with him?

'No, why should she be?' Seb demanded sharply.

'No reason,' Charlotte pacified him. 'I was just hoping...thinking...that it would be nice to see her.'

Normally her teasing and almost maternal probings would have been something he could have sidestepped with ease but today, after last night, it was activating pain cells he hadn't known he was capable of possessing. Just the sound of Katie's name was enough to produce a series of flash cards inside his brain.

Katie wearing just that damned towel. Katie her mouth swollen from his kiss. Katie reaching out to touch him. Katie as *he* touched *her*... Katie...

'Dad...where *are* you?'

Collecting himself he frowned down at Charlotte.

'Are you sure you're well enough to be discharged?'

'Ask the doc if you don't believe me,' she retaliated flippantly.

An hour later, having spoken with the duty doctor, the admissions staff and, in addition, having insisted on seeing the specialist in charge of the ward, Seb acknowledged that Charlotte had been right when she claimed that she was in perfect health.

'Dad, you're over-protective. You're practically Neanderthal,' she said as they finally left the ward.

'I'm your *father*,' Seb reminded her tersely looking at her in bafflement as she suddenly gave him a smile and hugged him.

'Yes, I know,' Charlotte conceded. 'But when the time comes when I finally meet a man...*the* man, Dad,' she emphasised with a sidelong look at him and a soft pink tinge to her skin, 'There's no way that I'm going to tell *you* about it. At least not until afterwards.' Her skin colour deepened a little more betrayingly as she added defensively, 'You'll terrify him.'

'Good,' Seb told her, but her semi-teasing words had set off a chain of thoughts of his own and there was no way he could share them with her.

The man she had said, meaning quite plainly the man who would be her first lover. Charlotte and her peers looked on sex as a responsibility that had to be treated with caution and respect and that, of course, was a legacy of the tainted inheritance other generations had left them.

He had been Katie's first lover. What would Jon Crighton think of him if he knew? Jon would not love his daughter any less than Seb loved Charlotte and Jon Crighton thought that he and Katie were a pair, a couple.

If he were to disappear out of Katie's life now, what

would Jon Crighton think of him? Would he think that he had used Katie, betrayed her, abandoned her? Would he condemn him as being every bit as bad as the worst of his Cooke ancestors? Would Seb be tarred by the same brush as them, a man totally without morals, without any kind of finer feelings?

'Dad… Dad…' Abruptly he realised that Charlotte was talking to him. 'Dad, are you okay?' Charlotte asked him in concern. 'You were miles away again…'

'I was thinking about…something…' Seb told her quickly.

'Something or *someone*?' Charlotte suggested, her face breaking into a wide smile when he wasn't quite quick enough to hide his reaction.

'I *knew* it. It is Katie, isn't it? You do love her, don't you, Dad? Oh, I'm so pleased,' Charlotte said hugging him excitedly. 'But just don't expect me to be a bridesmaid and dress in a pink tulle meringue.' Charlotte pulled a face. 'Okay, I know, Katie has far too much taste to want me to wear anything so uncool.'

'You're running ahead of the game,' Seb admonished her gently, changing the subject determinedly by telling her, 'Come on, let's get you back to Manchester.'

'Manchester! No way!' Charlotte announced firmly. 'I'm finishing my field trip first.'

They argued for several minutes but, in the end, Seb was forced to concede defeat and acknowledge that Charlotte was right to insist on continuing with her field trip.

'I'm an adult now, Dad,' she reminded him. 'And even if *I* wasn't… I love it that you are so protective of me, but sometimes I have to be allowed to feel the pain you know. It's called living.'

'Tell me about it,' Seb advised her sardonically.

*   *   *

'So what are you going to do when you get home?' Louise asked Katie. They were at the airport waiting for Katie's return flight.

'You mean *after* I've called a meeting in Haslewich's town square to explain why Seb and I are *not* an item?' Katie replied ruefully.

'Sorry about that,' Louise apologised. 'If I hadn't said anything…'

'It's not *your* fault,' Katie reassured her. '*I* should have had the courage to tell you the truth.'

'…and I should have realised that you were holding back. At least something good's come out of all this,' Louise murmured.

Their shared confidences had brought them closer than Katie could ever remember them being, closer and on a much more equal footing. With Gareth and Nick away, they had spent their first evening together exchanging confidences and swapping memories of their shared growing-up years, talking long into the night but returning again and again to the extraordinariness of the circumstances surrounding the way they had both come to realise where their true feelings lay.

On the final day of Katie's visit Gareth had returned home and it had been the most natural and the easiest thing in the world for Katie to go up to him and give him a sisterly hug and kiss.

She had known then when she did so, the fantasy, the *fear* that had gripped her for so long had gone. Gareth meant nothing to her apart from the fact that he was Louise's husband.

'It isn't over with Seb yet,' Louise reminded her.

'Yes, it is,' Katie responded fiercely, adding gently, 'I know that for my sake you'd love this to have a happy ending—for Seb to love *me*—but it isn't going to happen

Lou. You said yourself that Gareth told you that he had loved you that first time you were lovers even though *you* hadn't known it at the time. But Seb *doesn't* love me...'

'How do *you* know that?'

'Because *if* he did, he could have told me so,' Katie pointed out softly. 'Gareth *couldn't* tell you because you'd told him you loved someone else.'

'I hear what you're saying, but I still think you're wrong,' Louise insisted firmly.

'*Don't* Lou,' Katie begged her, her eyes suddenly darkening with pain. 'Don't give me any hope, all it's going to do is to make things worse.'

Louise saw the pain in her twin's eyes and hugged her tightly before reminding her,

'It won't be long before we come over...'

'...for Gramps' party, the one *I'm* supposed to produce Seb at for his inspection,' Katie replied dryly.

As she gave her a final hug, Louise sent up a private mental prayer for her sister's happiness, waiting until the last minute to thrust a prettily wrapped package into her sister's hand.

'What is it?' Katie asked her in surprise.

'It's the dress...the one we saw in the boutique window—the ''for Seb's eyes only'' dress. Remember?' Louise told her. 'I went back to get it when I told you I had to get a parking ticket for the car. I knew you wouldn't buy it yourself...'

'You knew right,' Katie told her feelingly and then, remembering the cost of the silky sensual slip she protested, 'You shouldn't have, Lou... There's no way I can ever wear it.'

'Of course you will.... Wear it for the family gathering,' Louise told her.

'What?'

'I dare you,' Louise challenged her wickedly, adding, 'You'd better go, otherwise you're going to miss your flight.'

Without giving Katie any chance to respond she gave her a little push and then stood watching her until she had disappeared.

CHAPTER NINE

'AND SO, if you would face the Court please and tell the jury exactly what you saw on the night of the eighteenth of October last year...'

Katie closed her eyes and tried to concentrate on what the witness who had just taken the stand was saying.

The delay in the jury reaching a verdict in a case in which Olivia had been acting had resulted in Katie having to take over from her at the last minute on another case being heard at Chester's Crown Court which had been brought forward. Although in many ways she was grateful to have the excuse for having to spend several days in Chester while the case was being heard, and therefore not having to run the risk of bumping into Seb, Katie was forced to admit that she was finding it hard to give her work her full attention; to blank Seb out of her mind completely.

'The Court will rise.'

Automatically Katie stood up. The judge had declared a recess. It was hot and stuffy in the courtroom despite the whir of the fans, and she was glad to be able to go outside and breathe in some fresher unrecycled air.

Her head had started to ache, a tight band of pain gripping her forehead. There was a chemist's shop close to the court, so she crossed the road and made her way towards it.

There was a queue at the counter and as she waited to be served she looked absently around. The array of drugs on sale was bewildering. Out of the corner of her eye Katie caught sight of a display of condoms and contraceptive products alongside pregnancy testing kits.

'You never know,' Louise had told her during their late night heart-to-heart. 'You may have already conceived Seb's child...'

'I haven't,' Katie had told her immediately and positively. 'Don't ask me how I know. I just *know*, but even if I *had*...that would be something, wouldn't it?' she had added sardonically. 'Having to tell the family that I'm pregnant and that Seb doesn't love me. Not that they'll need much telling about that. After all it will be pretty obvious I should imagine when I turn up at Gramps's "do" without him.'

She reached the till and paid for her headache tablets. Quite how she knew so positively that she wasn't carrying Seb's child she had no idea, she just knew that the gypsy woman had got it wrong, there wasn't going to be any baby... Any little boy so like his father... At least not for her.

It was a perfect afternoon as Katie drove back to Haslewich, the Welsh hills sharply clear against the skyline, the rich fields of the Cheshire plains laid out before her. Roman soldiers and merchants had once crossed this plain on their way from their port at Chester to the salt mines of Northwich, Nantwich, Middlewich and Haslewich. Salt mining had been the principal industry of the area along with farming right down through the centuries. Until the introduction of frozen and refrigerated foods, salt had been the only way that meat could be stored and safely preserved. Now the old workings had been turned into a museum and a tourist attraction. There was a local story that, during the Civil War, when the area had been heavily fought over by the rival

Cavalier and Roundhead forces, a certain very famous royal fugitive, the Stuart prince who would ultimately be King Charles II, had taken refuge in Haslewich's mines, but it had never actually been proved.

At her own suggestion, instead of returning to her own apartment, Katie drove over to her parents' where she had arranged to spend the night so that she would be on hand from early in the morning to help her mother and Maddy with their preparations for Ben's party.

As she walked in her mother's kitchen she was welcomed by the warm scent of baking and as Jenny enveloped her in a hug and asked her how her court case had gone, Katie thrust away the image that had been tormenting her all the way home of walking up to her apartment to find Seb waiting there for her with open arms.

But of course, that was never going to happen.

Over supper she chatted with her parents about her visit with Louise and the recent concluded court case.

She'd met with Max while she'd been in Chester and he'd confided to her, 'It looks very much as though I'm going to be elevated to the ranks of Queen's Counsel.'

'Oh Max,' Katie had beamed with sisterly pride. 'That's wonderful.'

'Well, it should help to cheer Gramps up a bit,' Max had agreed. 'I've talked it over with Maddy and we've both agreed that I should tell him during the party.'

'So that he can boast about it to everyone who's there,' Katie had teased, adding truthfully, 'Max, he will be so thrilled, this is what he's always wanted, to be able to claim a member of his own immediate family has those all important initials after his name—Max Crighton, QC. Oh Max…' She had hugged him excitedly and then shared the bottle of champagne that Luke had insisted on opening in their chambers when Max confessed to him that he hadn't been able to resist telling her his good news.

'You deserve it, Max,' Luke assured him and the two men had exchanged such a look of warmth and respect that Katie had felt her eyes start to fill with emotional tears.

'I've already told the folks,' Max had added to Katie just before she left.

'They will be thrilled,' Katie said.

'Yes,' Max agreed, and then giving her a wry look he had added, 'but like me, they feel that what I've got with Maddy and the children is of far more value.'

Katie had hugged him again knowing how much soul-searching and pain had been endured by both Max and Maddy before they had reached the loving intimacy of the marriage they now shared.

Now, seated at the table with her parents, Katie reflected that at least Max's news would take the pressure off her. With Max's elevation to boast about, her grandfather was hardly likely to concern himself with her relationship—or lack of it—with Seb. The female members of the family had never been accorded or merited as much importance in her grandfather's eyes as the males and for once Katie was happy to let that be so.

'Have you seen Seb since you got back?' her mother was asking her in a little concern now. 'You must have missed one another this last week...'

'I...' Now was her chance—her golden opportunity—to tell her parents the truth, Katie recognised, but as she took a deep breath ready to do so the phone rang and her mother got up from the table and hurried out of the room to answer it.

Before she returned, Max's wife Maddy had arrived

to drop off the fruit that Jenny needed to fill the tart cases she had been baking and then, within the hour, Maddy was on her way back to Queensmead where various members of the family were going to be staying for the weekend. Then Louise, Gareth and Nick had arrived and any chance Katie might have had to talk to her parents in private had gone.

'Well, that's the last batch of food delivered to Queensmead and it's time for us to get ourselves ready,' Louise announced, deftly removing the chocolaty crumbs her son was about to scrunch into her clean outfit.

'I can't wait to see you in that dress,' she enthused to Katie who immediately looked down at the floor, causing Louise to stop what she was doing and demand determinedly,

'You *are* going to wear it, aren't you, Katie?'

'I can't,' Katie protested. 'It's not…it's too…anyway, I don't have it here with me, it's at the apartment and there isn't time…'

'Lou,' Katie protested as her twin immediately reached for Katie's handbag and deftly extracted her keys, telling her in a voice that brooked no argument, 'There *is* time. I shall *make* time, and you my dear darling twin will wear it. Gareth,' she called over her shoulder to her husband who had just walked into the kitchen with Jon, 'You're going to have to wash and change Nick. His things are all laid out on the bed upstairs…'

'Louise,' Katie protested but it was too late, her sister was already out of the doorway and heading for hers and Gareth's rented car.

*　　*　　*

Seb frowned as he put down the telephone receiver. He had just rung Katie's flat for the fifth time without getting any reply that morning.

It had only been when he had telephoned the office and spoken with Olivia that he had discovered that Katie had returned from an unplanned visit to Brussels and then had virtually gone straight to court in Chester.

Was it a set of freak circumstances that was preventing him from being able to speak with her or was she *deliberately* avoiding him? Today was the date set for her grandfather's party—an event to which *he* was supposed to be escorting her—at least according to Guy.

Oh yes, he had enough, and to spare, practical reasons for needing to see Katie, but it wasn't those that were causing the aching longing which had taken over not just his emotions but his thoughts and time as well. Like a series of vivid flashbacks he kept getting mental images of the night they had made love, images which tormented every one of his five senses.

Broodingly he wondered what Katie herself was thinking and feeling. Did she regret what had happened? Did she blame him for it...hate him for it? Was she avoiding him out of embarrassment or anger? Did she... Did he really need to ask himself those questions he derided himself bitterly? He only had to remember what he had said to her before they had made love, the accusations he had made, the anger he had shown. But once they had touched, kissed, held one another... There was no point in him staying here, he decided, he might as well go out.

Louise was just crossing the hallway to Katie's flat when Seb opened his own front door.

'Katie...' he began and then stopped as he realised his mistake and Louise, who had seen the hope and longing flare quickly in his eyes only to die when he saw *her,* made a mental promise to herself that her twin would most definitely wear her new dress even if she herself had to dress her in it and drag her forcibly to the party.

'Katie's at home helping my mother get ready for Gramps's party,' Louise told him easily.

'Yes. Yes, of course. I...er...how is she?' Seb asked lamely.

Louise looked at him. Although they were identical twins, Seb knew that he could never mistake Louise for her twin. Katie was special, unique, she was...

'If you're *really* concerned, if you *really* care...' Louise emphasised, 'Then perhaps you should tell her so,' she suggested firmly.

Seb frowned.

Had Katie discussed what had happened between them with her twin? It seemed out of character for her. He knew instinctively that she was a very private and even reserved person, but twins shared a relationship and an intimacy that went far beyond that shared by non-twin siblings.

Louise brandished the elegant carrier bag she was holding.

'Katie's dress...for the party...' she told him conversationally, adding more pointedly and not entirely truthfully, 'She bought it in Brussels to wear today. For you...'

She was taking a huge risk, Louise knew that, and even worse she was not the one she was doing the risk taking for. If she had got it wrong and Seb did not care... If he was merely being polite...if what had happened between the two of them *had* simply been an impulsive act of the moment with no emotional importance in it for him, but no...there had been no mistaking that uncertain moment when he had asked about Katie, the very way he had been there, wanting to ask about her.

'The party starts at three,' she told him quietly, and then before he could say anything she hurried towards the lift.

Back at her parents' home Louise made no mention of seeing Seb much less of having spoken with him. Instead, she bundled Katie upstairs ignoring her protests that the dress was far too over the top for the nature of the event, pausing only to kiss Gareth as he emerged from their bedroom holding Nick.

'Mmm...you both smell wonderful,' she told him, adding impishly, 'Baby powder is soooo sexy on a man...'

'Lou, I can't *possibly* wear this,' Katie wailed. 'You can see right through it.'

'No you can't, it's got a nude slip, you just think you can...'

'That's what I mean,' Katie told her despairingly. 'It looks as though I haven't, as though I'm not...it's...'

'It's provocative and sexy and you look stunning in it,' Louise told her firmly.

She *did* look stunning in it Katie acknowledged as Louise determinedly turned her round to the mirror and commanded,

'Look...yes, I *know* you can see through it, but like I said, all you can actually see through to is the lining. Yes, I *know* it's flesh-coloured but look, it isn't as though you're showing masses of cleavage, not with that neat little round neck-hugging neckline, and, in fact, the only bits of you that are really bare are your arms and legs...'

'Maybe, but everyone will think that *all* of me...'

'Let them,' Louise interrupted her and then said with quiet sincerity, 'Katie, it looks wonderful on you. You *must* wear it. It makes you look…it makes you look like you should look…'

As she gave Louise an old-fashioned glance Louise shook her head and said, 'No, not like that. Yes, all right, it *is* sexy, but it's also stylish, elegant and sensual, not sleazy as you seem to be trying to say. There's nothing cheap or sleazy about it…or about you…

'Come on, it's time we went down, otherwise we're going to be late. Oh no,' she added when Katie told her that she needed to get her car keys, 'You don't think for one minute that I'm going to let you out of my sight, much less into your own car so that you can sneak back to your apartment and get changed behind my back. You're coming with us…come on…'

Queensmead was a big house with plenty of spare bedrooms which was just as well, Maddy had told Jenny, because they were certainly going to need them to put up all those members of the family who wanted to stay overnight.

'And when you add in all the children…it's just as well that most of them are still small enough to share their parents' rooms.'

As Katie walked into Queensmead's drawing room she could see what Maddy had meant, large though the room was, it was packed, filled with people.

Saul and Tullah were standing with their children talking with Saul's parents. Luke and Bobbie were in another group which included James, Luke's brother, their two sisters and their families and their parents.

'Looks like there's a full turn-out from the Chester

contingent of the Crightons,' Louise remarked to Katie as they stood together just inside the doorway.

'Mmm...that's definitely going to make Gramps's day,' she began, thinking of how pleased their grandfather would be at being able to boast to the two cousins he had always secretly felt he had had to compete with, of Max's good news, but Louise who didn't as yet know, gave her a puzzled look.

Bobbie, Luke's American wife who had just caught sight of the twins, was waving to them and, detaching herself from her own family group, came over, bringing her children with her.

'Wow...love the dress,' she approved as she studied Katie appraisingly. 'It is just soooo sexy...'

As Katie coloured up Louise groaned and then laughed, 'Don't tell her *that*. I've just spent the last hour convincing her that it isn't...'

'*I* never said you'd succeeded,' Katie pointed out dryly.

'So...' Bobbie teased her gently, 'Where is he?'

Katie knew perfectly well who the 'he' Bobbie meant was and she closed her eyes as a wave of sharp pain clawed her.

Louise was nudging her, warning, 'Katie... Katie...' causing her to open them again but the words of protest she had been about to deliver to her twin were lost when she saw Seb standing framed in the open doorway.

Even among the collective force of her male Crighton relatives, all of them tall, all of them dark and all of them extremely good looking, Seb stood out as she slowly scanned him. Katie avidly allowed her starved senses full rein to enjoy themselves and then Seb turned his head and saw her.

Katie sucked in her breath. The way he was looking

at her made her feel—made her think…made her *believe*… Her heart was pounding heavily, the interested massed ranks of her family faded into total oblivion. Seb was still looking at her and in his eyes she could see… She saw his lips form her name and then he was moving towards her. At her side Louise gave her a firm push in Seb's direction and somehow she was taking one step forward and then another and all the time he was looking at her with 'that' look.

Seb was used to large families. His own was huge, but the Crightons were a family apart, or so Ben Crighton liked to think, and as he stood looking into the packed drawing room Seb could see why. But there was only one person there *he* really wanted to see. Quickly he searched the room and then he found her, standing next to her sister, wearing a dress that made her look as ethereal as a wood sprite, as delicate and fragile as a piece of thistledown, as… He caught his breath as he saw the way she was looking at him, her whole heart in her eyes.

'Katie…' he breathed her name and the crowd of people separating them seemed to part as though by magic.

'Katie…'

As he reached her and said her name Katie closed her eyes unable to stop the ecstatic shudder of happiness that shook her and then she was in his arms and he was holding her, kissing her.

Eagerly she returned his kiss, her lips parting hungrily as she clung to him.

'Seb.' She gasped his name.

'I've missed you,' she heard him groan. '*Why* didn't you ring…get in touch? Why am I wasting time talking? Why are *we* wasting time here?' he muttered thickly against her mouth, 'And why are you wearing that damned dress that makes me want to...'

'Seb,' Katie protested, pink cheeked, but smiling as she placed a cautionary finger against his lips. His hand curled around her wrist and he kissed her finger, nibbling tenderly on it while his thumb monitored the frantic thud of her pulse. With give-away bemusement in her love-dazed eyes, she reminded him shakily, 'There are children here and...'

Children...a sudden shockingly explicit look darkened his eyes so that they smouldered and burned.

Shielding her from everyone else with his body he told her quietly, 'You could be carrying my child...our child...'

Katie couldn't help it, she gasped out loud, her whole body reacting to the intimacy of what he was saying.

'No, I don't think so,' she told him. 'Not...'

'...not this time,' he suggested.

Not *this* time... Katie felt as though she might faint she was so incandescent with happiness and disbelief. How *could* this be happening? How could her emotional skies have gone from darkest grey to brightest blue and all within the space of a single breath, all because of one specific look?

'I never thought you'd be here,' she whispered. 'I was going to tell everyone that there's been a misunderstanding, apologise to them for not saying anything before. I never dreamed...'

'No,' Seb was giving her a very rueful look. 'Did you think then that what we shared together was so commonplace and mundane...'

Katie shook her head immediately.

'Oh no...no...it was...' She paused and looked at him, her eyes, her gaze direct but a little shy. 'It was wonderful, Seb…magical…something I never imagined. It frightened me a little to go from not knowing, from not realising just what I felt to recognising that all that anger, all that aggression I'd been feeling towards you was really nothing more than a barrier I'd built up because I was afraid to acknowledge what I really felt.'

'And what do you really feel?' Seb asked her.

Katie looked at him. The look she could see in his eyes was telling her to trust in him, to believe in him, to have the courage to be honest with him.

She took a deep breath.

'I… I love you,' she told him huskily.

As she said the words she felt his fingers tighten around her wrist.

'Let's get out of here,' he told her thickly. 'What I want to say to you…what I want to *do* with you…' Katie heard him groan. 'That damned dress,' he whispered vehemently. 'It's driving me crazy…*you're* driving me crazy, Katie Crighton, crazy with longing, crazy with need, crazy with love…'

'We can't go yet,' Katie protested unconvincingly. Her relatives had discreetly drifted away leaving the two of them surrounded by a protective moat of empty space and silence, but…

'If you don't stop looking at me like that I'm going to have to make love to you right here and now and be damned to the consequences,' Seb growled. '*That* will impress your grandfather, won't it? I must be more of a Cooke than I've ever realised and I'm certainly enough of one not to give a damn who knows or sees just how much I want you, Katie…and enough of one to carry you off, steal you away with me as my notorious ancestor was reputed to have done with *his* lady love.'

'Seb,' Katie protested breathlessly. 'Just let me go and say my farewells to Gramps and then we can go.'

'I think you're going to have to do a bit more than just wish him farewell,' Seb told her wryly, 'at least if the looks he's been throwing in our direction for the last few minutes are anything to go by.'

'Give me a few minutes to explain to him,' Katie suggested, 'and then I'll introduce you to him.'

Nodding his head, Seb slowly released her hand and then, just as she was about to slip away, reached for her possessively and kissed her briefly but very passionately. 'A few minutes,' he warned her. 'That's all. You and I have got a lot of lost time to make up.'

'Mmm…a whole week of it,' Katie teased him blissfully before wriggling out of his arms and heading towards her grandfather.

Tenderly Seb watched her. She was his joy, his future, his hope, his love and he didn't care who knew it. And he intended to prove it to her very, very thoroughly and protractedly indeed just as soon as he could get her to himself. That dress… He closed his eyes as he imagined touching her through it, kissing her and then opened them again as close at hand he heard a woman's voice saying quietly, 'My goodness me, what a change in Katie… I hardly recognised her.'

Alison Ford raised her eyebrows a little as she listened to her sister Rachel. Their father, Henry Crighton, was Ben's cousin and their brother Luke was married to Bobbie, Ruth Crighton's American granddaughter. Nearly two decades older than Louise and Katie, they were both married with growing families.

'Mmm…quite a change from the way she looked at Louise's wedding,' Alison agreed.

'Yes indeed. It's never been mentioned, but my private suspicion was that her feelings for Gareth weren't just those of a sister-in-law...'

'You mean she was in love with him?'

As the two women started to move away from Seb their voices faded but the damage was done. Fiercely he searched the room until he found who he was looking for. Gareth, Louise's husband, and there, right beside him was Katie, looking up at him, smiling at him, standing so close to him that she was within easy kissing distance of him... *His* Katie...

Seb was not by nature a jealous man but the sight of Katie standing so intimately close to Gareth after what he had just overheard and while his own love for her was so newly declared and his ego so fragile and vulnerable, overwhelmed all his logic and self-control.

How dare Gareth stand so close to his beloved? How dare he talk so intimately to her? How could he possibly resist her especially when she was wearing such a dress, a dress that would make a saint want...?

Katie chuckled appreciatively as Gareth reached the end of the amusing anecdote he had been relating to her. It amazed her how much she was enjoying this new relationship she had developed with him, the sense of camaraderie, of sisterly closeness and warmth which she could tell he happily reciprocated. She felt no sense of discomfort or self-consciousness in his presence now. The Gareth she had believed she loved had simply been a creation of her own imagination, an impossibly one-dimensional and, yes, virtually sexless figure who bore absolutely no resemblance to the real Gareth at all.

'I thought you said you wanted to say goodbye to your grandfather.'

Katie jumped as out of nowhere, or so it seemed, Seb suddenly materialised at her side, somehow or other managing to stand in between her and Gareth, his eyes hard and angry, his voice unmistakably harsh.

'Yes. I did... I do... but...'

'But you found someone more...interesting to talk to...' Seb suggested grittily to her.

Katie stared at him.

'I...'

'Oh, you don't have to explain to me,' Seb told her firmly. 'I've just heard a very enlightening conversation.'

Out of the corner of her eye Katie could see the curious looks they were attracting. Gareth who was standing the closest to them was starting to frown a little bit.

'Seb,' she protested, but he ignored her, propelling her towards the door.

'*Who* was it you were really saving your virginity for Katie?' he demanded. 'Not me, that's for sure.'

'Seb,' Katie protested again just as soon as they were on their own in the hallway.

'It was *Gareth*, wasn't it?' he demanded, ignoring her. 'Gareth, your brother-in-law!' he emphasised. 'You're in love with him. Don't bother denying it. Is *that* why you're wearing that dress? For *him*... Hoping that he'd...'

'You're jealous,' Katie gasped as she saw the emotions darkening his eyes. 'And...and you're wrong... I don't love Gareth...'

'Gareth—what?' Seb demanded savagely. 'Gareth doesn't *want* you because he's married to your twin... Well that certainly wasn't the impression I just got. He was looking at you as though...'

'Seb, you've got it all wrong,' Katie protested swiftly.

'No, *you're* the one who's got things wrong. If you think for one moment that I'm going to let another man—*any* other man come between us. I love you Katie and I'm pretty damn sure that you love me, no matter how much you might think that another man… Just give me a chance to prove how good it could be for us, Katie, that's all I ask, and I promise you…'

He stopped when he saw the searchingly solemn-eyed look she was giving him and then, taking a deep breath, he decided to use his trump card, the card he had promised himself he would never play; the one that came so loaded with emotional dynamite that he'd have to be either a fool or desperate to use it—or maybe even both.

'Remember what the gypsy said,' he told her gruffly. 'It was *my* baby she saw you with, Katie.'

His baby… Katie stared at him, his jealousy, his passion, his determination, all of them were so unexpected, so very much the opposite of what she had assumed to be his feelings towards her, his indifference towards her that she still couldn't quite totally absorb them.

His baby… Her heart and with it her doubts melted in the sweet hot-honeyed tide of love that spread through her.

'No,' she corrected him softly. 'Not *your* baby, Seb…' The look in his eyes made her reach out impulsively to touch him reassuringly, her fingertips resting on his arm, hard and tensed beneath the cloth of his jacket as though he was both fearing her rejection and bracing himself for it.

'*Our* baby, Seb… *Our* baby. *Yours* and *mine*.'

As she looked at him she saw him swallow and then heard him say in a thick emotional voice,

'Come on, let's get out of here…'

In the drawing room Max had just given Ben Crighton his news. Through the open doorway Katie could see her grandfather's face quite plainly. Max's news had totally eclipsed anything she might have said to Gramps or anything he might have wanted to say to her—thankfully.

Breathing a small sigh of thanks to her brother she looked up into Seb's face.

'Yes,' she agreed softly. 'Let's...'

'Have I told you just how much I love you...just how wonderful you are, how gorgeous, how adorable, how sexy and...'

'Mmm...but you can tell me all over again if you like,' Katie said happily as she snuggled deeper into his side.

The late-afternoon sun shining in through the window of his apartment brushed their naked bodies with a soft gold wash of colour. Seb's skin was much darker than hers, his body hair dark and silky.

Idly she stroked her fingers through it and then leaned over teasingly, kissing one of his nipples and then the other.

'Do you know what you're doing?' Seb growled, his growl turning to an urgent low groan of reaction as she tugged sensually on the small hard nub of flesh, her palm spread flat on the concave plane of his belly.

'I never really loved Gareth, you know,' she told him gently a few minutes later as she propped herself up on one elbow and looked lovingly down into his face. 'I just thought I did, but the Gareth I imagined I loved never really existed, he was just someone I'd created in my own head, and as for you being jealous of him...' She gave him a searching look and then said quietly, *'You've* been married, Seb. You must have loved Sandra once...and...'

Quickly Seb shook his head.

'We thought we loved one another but it was just an infatuation, something which by rights we should have got out of our systems with a few nights of experimental sex, but I was too strait-laced, too aware of my Cooke heritage to do that. Sandra and I should never have married and we certainly should never have had a child. I *do* feel guilty about that, about not being there for Charlotte when she was growing up, but when Sandra told me that she felt it was for the best that Charlotte didn't have any kind of contact with me rather than be torn between the two of us I felt that she was right and then she married George and to all intents and purposes he became Charlotte's father.'

'That must have been hard for you,' Katie said gently, 'knowing that another man was taking your place.'

'It wasn't always easy,' Seb agreed wryly, 'but for Charlotte's sake...' He stopped. 'When I first got in touch with her I was terrified that she might be disappointed in me, that I wouldn't live up to her expectations and that I might somehow have damaged her by not being there for her, but she's just about the most well-adjusted human being I know...'

'Mmm...' Katie agreed and then asked him a little hesitantly, 'How will she feel, do you suppose, about us?'

Seb looked at her and then shook his head gravely, 'That's going to be a problem, I'm afraid,' he told her solemnly.

Katie's heart lurched. 'It...it is?'

'Mmm... She's already told me that there's absolutely, totally no way she will ever...' He paused while Katie looked anxiously at him. 'Ever...' he continued dramatically, 'wear a bridesmaid's dress that makes her look like a pink meringue...'

'What?' Katie glared at him and then burst out laughing.

'She thinks you're wonderful,' Seb told her softly, 'and she can't *wait* for us to provide her with another clutch of half siblings...'

'Oh Seb,' Katie whispered, her eyes full of emotional tears.

'Oh Seb, what?' Seb repeated equally emotionally, but Katie couldn't make any rational vocal response because he was kissing her, pressing her back against the pillows, pinioning her arms in a tender mock-masterful lover's embrace as he kissed her, slowly and softly at first and then with increasing passion and urgency as his body hardened and Katie gave a low female moan of arousal deep in her throat. The soft rose-pink colour staining her breasts now didn't come from the dying sun but from the slow sensual suckle of Seb's mouth. As he kissed the soft curve of her belly Katie arched frantically beneath him. His hand caressed her thigh and then tenderly touched her sex. Katie moaned out loud.

'We shouldn't be doing this,' Seb reminded her with a soft groan as she turned towards him, 'Not without...' But Katie was already touching him, stroking him and the urge to bury himself deep inside her was far too strong for him to resist.

Later, lying in Seb's arms, Katie gave a blissful sigh and told him softly,

'I saw him...just now, when...he was so beautiful, Seb...'

'Yes, I know,' he agreed quietly, 'I saw him too.'

They looked at one another sharing the awe of what they had both experienced.

'He looked so like you,' Katie told him tremulously.

Seb frowned.

'No,' he corrected her, '*He* looked like *you*.'

Katie's eyes widened.

'Twins,' she whispered chokily, 'We're going to have twins. Oh Seb… Seb…'

'Mmm…' Seb breathed as she kissed him. 'Careful…it could be triplets…'

Katie laughed.

'There are no triplets in the Crighton family,' she mock scolded him.

'We'll have to get married…and soon,' Seb warned her.

Katie pursed her lips and pretended to frown.

'I mean it, Katie,' Seb told her fiercely. 'This isn't a "let's live together and see how it works out" thing for me. You're the woman I love and it's a "forever love" for me…'

'…and for me,' Katie assured him happily.

'A quiet simple wedding,' Seb continued, stopping when Katie started to laugh.

'No…no way can we do that,' she told him joyously. 'You're a Cooke and I'm a Crighton, Seb, and the whole town is going to want to see us married. It's just as well Haslewich has such a large church.'

'Mmm…but does it have a large *font*,' Seb murmured before drawing her down against his body and then silencing whatever reply she might have made with a long sensual kiss.

EPILOGUE

'IT'S just as well that Haslewich has such a large church,' Jenny Crighton told her husband, unconsciously echoing Katie's own comment to Seb.

'Mmm... I know they're in love, but does everything have to happen in such a rush?' Jon protested ruefully, stopping when he saw the look Jenny was giving him.

'Oh,' he exclaimed, 'I see...'

'Katie hasn't *said* anything,' Jenny warned him, 'but Louise is pretty sure, and you know how it is with them, being twins...they seem to share a special bond and...' Jenny broke off as she saw her husband's expression. Gently she touched his arm. Her Jon was a twin himself, even if he and his brother David weren't in contact with one another anymore.

'Your father still believes that ultimately David will return home.'

'Yes, I know,' Jon agreed heavily. 'You know I had the oddest feeling when I went to Jamaica that...'

'...that what?' Jenny pressed him, but he was already shaking his head.

'Oh, nothing... So we've got another wedding to look forward to. Which reminds me, we're coming up to Olivia and Caspar's anniversary.'

Jenny started to frown.

'What is it?' Jon asked her.

185

'I don't know,' Jenny admitted. 'It's just that Olivia seems to be rather on edge at the moment.'

'Mmm…well, we are under a lot of pressure at the practice which, of course, is one of the reasons why I was so pleased when Katie agreed to join us. Which reminds me,' Jon joked, 'we're very definitely going to have to think about buying that dining room table you were telling me about!'

'The one that extends to seat twenty?' Jenny asked him. 'You said it was too big.'

'Mmm…that was before I'd added up the number of grandchildren our family is blessing us with.'

Jenny laughed and agreed. 'Yes, Katie was saying only last night that it's just as well the church has such a long aisle…for all the little bridesmaids she's going to have,' she explained. 'Close on a dozen at the last count.'

'A dozen!' Charlotte exclaimed, looking bemused when Katie outlined her wedding plans to her that same evening.

'Mmm…all of them dressed in little pink mini-meringues,' Katie told her solemnly, tongue-in-cheek.

'Like *what*?' Suddenly realising she was being teased, Charlotte burst out laughing.

'All right, I agree to take charge of them and to act as yours and Dad's support, but no *way* am I wearing pink or tulle.'

'No way,' Katie agreed, her eyes dancing with laughter and love.

'Oh, I'm so glad you and Dad have found one another,' Charlotte told her happily.

As Katie smiled at her and then looked across the

room to where Seb was watching them, her eyes sparkled with happiness and love.

'So am I...' she told Charlotte tenderly.

*   *   *   *   *

The Crighton family saga continues with
David Crighton's story

COMING HOME

Available soon.

Romance is just one click away!

online book **serials**

➢ *Exclusive* to our web site, get caught up in both the daily and weekly online installments of new romance stories.

➢ Try the Writing Round Robin. Contribute a chapter to a story created by our members. Plus, winners will get prizes.

romantic **travel**

➢ Want to know where the best place to kiss in New York City is, or which restaurant in Los Angeles is the most romantic? Check out our Romantic Hot Spots for the scoop.

➢ Share your travel tips and stories with us on the romantic travel message boards.

romantic reading **library**

➢ Relax as you read our collection of Romantic Poetry.

➢ Take a peek at the Top 10 Most Romantic Lines!

Visit us online at

www.eHarlequin.com
on Women.com Networks